'Suddenly Clo caught sight of a big white car speeding towards them from the left. She heard Eric swear and Beth scream as it hit them side-on. The next thing she knew, she was hanging upside down in her seat belt with broken glass everywhere...'

Although Clo escapes with only cuts and bruises, her sister Beth comes home in a wheelchair and life changes dramatically for both sisters.

At first guilty, then resentful, Clo's feelings change when she sees how others treat Beth. Clo knows her sister is still the same person inside, but because she's disabled others assume she's stupid. When the sisters discover how hard it is to get around town in a wheelchair, Clo sets out to change things.

Former actress, Rowena Edlin-White is now both a novelist and a poet. Her hobbies include browsing in bookshops and at markets, and hand-spinning and dyeing. She lives with her husband in Nottingham.

For my God-daughter, Daisy

To Joshua

Merry Christmas 2023
and a happy 2024!
Love Always
Janet, Everton
& Joel
xx

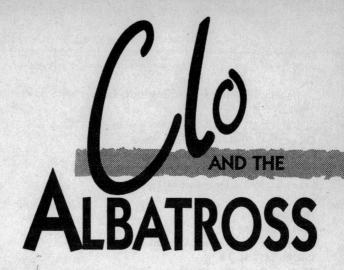

Clo AND THE ALBATROSS

Rowena Edlin-White

A LION BOOK

Published by
Lion Publishing plc
Sandy Lane West, Oxford, England
ISBN 0 7459 3462 5
Albatross Books Pty Ltd
PO Box 320, Sutherland, NSW 2232, Australia
ISBN 0 7324 1449 0

First edition 1996
First paperback edition 1997
10 9 8 7 6 5 4 3 2 1 0

A catalogue record for this book is available
from the British Library

Printed and bound in Great Britain

1

Chloe Olerenshaw sat brooding in the darkest corner of the end shelter by the lake in Brickfields Memorial Park. What was wrong with her? Half an hour ago she had been laughing and joking with her friend Ginny. Now, because of the remarks of a couple of old ladies, she was right down in the dumps again. She stared listlessly across the grey lake, a thin thirteen-year-old with wire-rimmed spectacles and straight brown hair tied in a skinny pony-tail. Some lines from Coleridge's 'Ancient Mariner' ran through her head:

> Alone, alone, all, all alone,
> Alone on a wide, wide sea!

But she wasn't alone, not entirely. Inevitably her eyes were drawn to her companion, a figure in a wheelchair silhouetted in the doorway. Her sister, Beth. Chloe narrowed her eyes in an attempt to fuzz out the girl and her chair.

'But it doesn't work,' she admitted silently, 'because she always *is* there, like a stranger, having to be carried and pushed and helped to do everything.'

It was painful to contrast this Beth with Beth as she used to be, once so active and alive.

'And here's me,' Chloe reflected bitterly, 'fit and healthy, but handicapped as well—by her! Mam says I should be thankful I escaped but I'm not, because I didn't. I don't feel thankful, I just feel trapped and lonely.'

And for the hundredth time she thought back to how it had happened.

Last November. Chloe, commonly known as Clo, was enjoying school, Rushworth Comprehensive. Beth was two years above her in Year 10, concentrating hard on sciences because she wanted to be a doctor, but also a rising star on the sports field. Clo preferred reading and drawing but Beth loved hockey, netball, swimming and, best of all, gymnastics. Clo loved to see her arch her body over the bar, then flip backwards through the air—as though she were made of elastic!

'That girl will go far, mark my words,' Miss Poole, the gym teacher, often remarked.

Clo thought Beth was like those beautiful, talented heroines in old-fashioned school stories—perfect—and was her greatest fan.

But Clo was good at other things; she was excited to have been given a part in the school production of *As You Like It*. She was only in Year 8 but she had attracted the attention of Miss Redmond, her English teacher.

'Why not audition for the part of Audrey?' she suggested. 'Shakespeare describes her as a simple country wench. It isn't a big part, but it can be very funny.'

Clo read the part aloud that night after school. She had to stand at one end of the gym while Miss Redmond and Mr James, the art teacher, sat at the other end.

'Great stuff, Chloe!' called Mr James when she had finished. 'But don't be tempted to over-do it; the less you do, the funnier it will be. Audrey is a complete innocent; she takes everything very seriously.'

'I see,' said Clo. 'Have I got the part then, Sir?'

'There's keen!' Mr James laughed.

'Wait and see when the cast list goes up tomorrow,' Miss Redmond said, 'but unofficially... I think you can start learning your part!'

Clo left the gym feeling elated but she didn't dare congratulate herself. Not yet.

She overheard Mr James say to Miss Redmond, 'She's a natural, that one, she'll bring the house down!'

At break next day Clo joined the eager crowd pressing round the Drama notice-board. She squeezed to the front and read: *Audrey—Chloe Olerenshaw, 2R.*

'Oh, goodie!' she exclaimed. 'I've got it!'

Janice Fisher, a friend of Beth's, looked down her nose. 'Oh, that's only a bit part,' she said, 'Rosalind is the best part and Jenny's playing her.'

Jenny Hall smiled and said, 'Give over, Janice! All the parts are good ones.'

'I don't mind,' Clo said happily, 'Audrey's a very funny part, Miss Redmond said so!'

Beth was practising netball outside in the yard. She seemed to bounce into the air without any effort at all, her bright blonde curls bouncing with her. Clo waited with an admiring group of Year 9s until her sister had finished, then told her the news.

6

'Good for you, kid!' Beth said, patting her on the back. 'I didn't know you'd auditioned for the play. You kept that quiet!'

'Well, I didn't want to say anything to Mam. She might have been disappointed if I hadn't got it in the end.'

Mam was really their granny; she and Eric, their step-grandad, had taken care of the girls since their mother had gone to America. She was delighted when Clo came home that night with her script.

'Well I never,' she exclaimed, 'a star gymnast in the family and now a budding actress!'

'It's only a little part, Mam,' Clo protested.

'They're often the most interesting, lovey,' Mam replied. 'I'm dead proud of you.'

'Mr James said I'd bring the house down—whatever that means,' Clo told her.

'He means you'll make 'em laugh until they bust!' said Eric, 'Eh, our Clo, I can hardly wait!'

Clo worked hard, practising her lines in front of the bedroom mirror when Beth was out training. She wanted to do well even if it was only two little scenes.

'Beth's always winning medals and breaking records and they're so pleased with her,' she thought, 'I'd like to do something they'd be proud of too.'

Then the accident happened. They had been to the Baths with Eric. Every Friday night he picked them up from school and they drove to the swimming pool a couple of miles away. Clo didn't like water much, it got in her ears and made her deaf and she couldn't see far without her spectacles; but she was happy to splash about in the shallow end while Eric and Beth raced each other against the clock.

Damp fog enveloped them as they left the Baths that particular night.

'Heck, I thought we'd have to call out the AA man just to find the car!' Eric laughed as they strapped themselves in, Beth in front, Clo in the back.

'I did seventy-five lengths tonight, Clo,' Beth said, matter-of-fact.

'Hey, that's more than a mile, isn't it?' Clo was impressed.

They didn't ask her how many *she'd* done—a puny six widths in the kiddies' end.

'How's your play going, Clo?' Eric asked. 'Will you know all your words by Christmas?'

'Oh I know all the lines, it's just getting them in the right places!'

'You're a caution, our Clo,' Eric chuckled, carefully turning right into Raglan Street where they lived.

Suddenly Clo caught sight of a big white car speeding towards them from the left. She heard Eric swear and Beth scream as it hit them side on.

The next thing she knew, she was hanging upside down in her seat belt with broken glass everywhere and a chaotic mixture of anxious voices, car-horns and police sirens filled her ears.

Eric's voice came from somewhere miles away, 'Hold on there, my lass, we'll soon have you out!'

Then they were in an ambulance, screeching through the traffic to the hospital. Mam was there—what with the crash being so near home and her being a nurse she had run out to see if she could help, only to find, to her horror, that the injured were her own family.

Clo was sent home that night. She wasn't hurt, only shaken up, but Beth was still unconscious in Rushworth General Hospital, where Eric worked as a porter.

'I'm right glad I wasn't on duty that night,' he said, 'I'd have died of shock to see one of you laying there on a stretcher.'

He had one wrist in plaster and a stiff collar round his neck and took over at home while Mam spent every minute she could at Beth's bedside.

Clo lay listlessly on the sofa, numb with shock. She didn't feel like eating and she couldn't read or watch television because her glasses had been broken in the crash.

On the third day, Eric removed her uneaten lunch and said quietly, 'Y'know something, lass, it'd do you good to have a good weep—get it out your system.'

But Clo just shook her head miserably.

'What right have I got to cry,' she thought, 'when Beth still hasn't come round?'

The fifth day after the accident Mam came home tired but happy to say that Beth had opened her eyes, though she still hadn't spoken.

'Never mind, it's a start, thank the Lord,' she said. 'Now our Clo, let's have a smile! Things are looking up and life goes on. Beth's on the road to recovery and we must get you back to school.'

8

She hugged Clo who managed a weak smile. By tea time she had found her appetite again and ate her egg and chips.

Later on Clo had a visitor, her teacher Miss Redmond.

'Sit yourself down now,' Eric said, leading her to the nicest armchair by the fire.

Clo felt a bit ashamed that Miss Redmond, who dressed so smartly and spoke poetry so beautifully, should see the shabby old flat they lived in. But Miss Redmond seemed to feel perfectly at home.

'I can't tell you what a shock this has been to us all, Chloe,' she said, 'but we're very relieved it wasn't worse. We think it's probably time you came back to school—you've missed two rehearsals already and we really do need our Audrey. What do you say, might we see you next week?'

The play! Clo had forgotten that!

'Oh yes, Miss,' she said, 'yes, of course I'll come back. After all,' she attempted a feeble joke, 'the show must go on!'

'That's my Chloe!' Miss Redmond laughed, accepting a cup of tea from Mam who smiled to hear Clo sound more like herself.

'Yes,' Mam said, 'I'm sure it would be best for her to get back to normal as soon as possible. She'll have her new glasses tomorrow so she'll be able to see the board.'

'And what news of Elisabeth?' Miss Redmond enquired.

'Improving, thank you, no bones broken and she's recovered consciousness but, well'—Mam glanced at Clo—'don't expect to see her back at school yet awhile. I'm afraid it could be a long job. They say she'll need a lot of care.'

'What a blessing you have the training to nurse her yourself,' Miss Redmond said.

'Yes indeed, and the good Lord gives us nothing that we're not fit to carry,' Mam answered firmly.

Clo turned her head away. It hadn't occurred to her that it might take a long time. After all, Beth hadn't broken anything. She'd imagined that after a week or so in bed, she'd be back at school, leaping about in the gym again.

'What's wrong with her?' she thought, suddenly frightened. 'And what's Mam going on about the good Lord for? What's good about a God who lets such horrible things happen to people, specially Beth?'

Miss Redmond patted Mam on the arm and smiled. 'Just what my mother always said, Mrs Appleby. Good-bye, Chloe—we look forward to seeing you on Monday.'

Clo smiled brightly but she was really only acting; she couldn't muster the enthusiasm for anything. How could she, when she now knew that Beth was going to be 'a long job'?

2

Back at school Clo found herself the centre of attention. Janice and Jenny came to her at break and gave her a Get Well card for Beth. They were clearly shocked.

Even bossy Janice was close to tears. 'It's awful, just awful,' she kept saying.

Clo thanked them in a flat, expressionless voice, unable to feel very much at all.

She perked up later as she made her way to the gym for a play rehearsal. She was greeted by Derek Gibson who was playing Touchstone.

'Hi, Chloe! Good to see you, I was getting a bit tired of acting to thin air!'

They didn't really act that night, just walked through their scenes while Miss Redmond told them where to move, and wrote these instructions in their scripts. After a while Clo found it hard to concentrate.

'Had enough, Chloe?' asked Miss Redmond.

'Sorry, Miss.'

'Not to worry, dear, you've had a long day. We'll finish there. See you both on Friday for the last scene.'

She gathered up her papers while Clo slowly put on her coat.

'Like a lift home?' she asked, when Derek was out of earshot.

'No thanks, Miss, Mam's coming for me. We're going up the General to see Beth.' Clo wasn't too happy about this.

'All right dear. Give Elisabeth my love.'

Miss Redmond watched her go. 'I must keep an eye on our Chloe,' she murmured.

As they approached the hospital Mam sensed Clo hanging back.

'What's up, lovey?'

'Mam, is she all... you know?'

Clo didn't know how to say it. She was afraid Beth might look like something out of the TV programme 'Casualty', with tubes and wires all over the place.

11

'She just looks like our Beth,' Mam reassured her, 'only... they had to cut her hair off to stitch the cuts in her head, so I'm afraid she's lost all her pretty curls.'

Clo was horrified.

'But she's got a bandage on, so you can't see anything, pet.' Mam knew Clo was squeamish about medical things. 'Good job you don't want to be a nurse!' she often joked.

But she didn't joke now, she squeezed Clo's hand and smiled. Clo tried to smile back but her mouth felt stiff.

They walked down miles of corridors until at last they reached Nightingale Ward. Beth was lying in a high bed; her eyes were open but she was very still and her face very white beneath the bandages.

One or two of the other patients called out to Mam, greeting her like an old friend. They called hello to Clo, too, but she just looked round nervously and didn't reply.

'Eh up, my lass!' said Mam, sitting on a chair by the bed and taking Beth's white hands in her own. 'Look who's here to see you—our Clo! Say hello to her, Clo.'

'Hi, Beth,' Clo managed. Then in a rush, 'I went back to school today and Janice and Jenny came and said how sorry they were about—you know—and sent you this.'

She pulled a crumpled envelope from her school bag.

'Oh, and Miss Redmond sends her love too.'

Beth's eyes flickered but she didn't reply.

Mam said, 'Why not open it for her, Clo love, and pop it on the locker where she can see it?'

Clo opened the envelope carefully and read the rather trite message on the card over and over again. Meanwhile Mam kept up a stream of chit-chat to the silent Beth, telling her what they were having for supper and all about life at 47a Raglan Street.

'Why on earth', Clo thought, 'is she going on about all those boring things when Beth isn't even listening?' She was glad when it was time to go.

As they left Mam explained, 'Beth's suffering from what they call a Reversible Brain Injury; there shouldn't be any permanent damage, but it sometimes takes quite a while to mend. Even though she isn't talking yet she can still hear us, and she needs to be kept in touch with everyday life—that's why I was gabbing on.'

Clo blushed. Mam was so good and wise, she always knew the right thing to do.

Every evening for the next few weeks Mam or Eric visited Beth; they were seldom at home together. This wasn't the comfortable routine Clo was used to, and it worried her. She and Beth had lived with Mam and Eric since she was five. Up until then they had been constantly on the move with their mother, so it had felt like coming home at last when they had climbed the stairs to the first-floor flat in Raglan Street. Mam had given up work to take care of them while they were little and had always encouraged and supported them; Clo relied on her. Pretty, athletic Beth had always been noticed and admired but it had taken Clo longer to find ways to express herself. She clowned around and did funny voices, embroidered pictures on her jumpers and painted jungle scenes on her trainers—you couldn't miss Clo in a crowd! Now she felt uneasy, unsure of everything she normally took for granted.

Rehearsals continued, and the little scenes with Derek soon got swamped by the rest of the play. Clo found herself walking through them mechanically. She did most things on auto-pilot these days, as if her body were going through the motions but her mind was somewhere else. Her attention wandered in class—sometimes she even fell asleep. Bed-time brought a sense of relief; she slept deeply till morning, when she dragged herself out of bed to go through it all again. She withdrew into herself and no longer fooled around for the benefit of her class-mates.

One night, after rehearsal, Miss Redmond called her back.

'Come and sit down, Chloe,' she said.

'What's up?' asked Mr James. 'I had high hopes of you as Audrey, I thought you'd have 'em rolling in the aisles. I know I told you not to over-do it but really, I think you've gone a bit too far the other way!'

Clo looked at her hands.

'I know they're only little scenes, but Shakespeare wouldn't have bothered putting them in if they weren't important, now would he? They are worth the effort, I promise you.'

Mr James wasn't cross, Clo could tell, just puzzled, and Miss Redmond was kind and inquiring.

'Sorry, Sir,' she said, 'I do love the part, honestly, and I was so looking forward to it, I learnt all my lines the first week, but...'

'But?' prompted Mr James.

'Since... since the accident, I just can't seem to, well, get into anything, I feel as if... I'm somewhere else a lot of the time,' she ended lamely.

Miss Redmond looked at her for a moment. 'Poor Chloe. Just because you escaped unhurt, people have forgotten you went through that awful experience too. It isn't surprising you feel out of it, as they say. Listen, if you really don't feel up to doing the part, say so now. We can easily rehearse somebody else in and no one will mind one bit.'

'On the other hand,' said Mr James, 'if you do decide to stay in the cast you're going to have to make an effort. Every part in a play, however small, is important, and if you just let it go by, you don't just let me and Miss Redmond down, you let yourself down and all the rest of the cast and...'

He paused for effect.

'... and most of all your audience who have paid their one-fifty, or whatever, to be entertained. D'you understand me, Chloe?'

No, she hadn't thought of it like that, that her lack of effort could affect so many people, and Mam and Eric were so looking forward to it. Mam was going to have to give up her job at an old people's home to look after Beth, and nobody had even mentioned Christmas. No, she couldn't let them down.

'Well, what'll it be?' asked Mr James. 'It's up to you. But whatever you choose, choose it whole-heartedly, no half measures, eh?'

Clo took a deep breath. 'Yes,' she said, 'I will do it and I'll do it well for... for all of you.'

'Bravo, Chloe! You'll do it all right, I know you will.'

'We'll do it together,' said Miss Redmond. 'You said it yourself, the show must go on!'

'Yes, Miss!' Clo grinned, and meant it.

She walked home through dark, frosty streets. What Mr James had said reminded her of something she'd once heard in Chapel. Mam went to Rushworth Methodist Church down Waterloo Road—always referred to as 'Chapel' by the older generation—and Beth and Clo used to go to Sunday School there. Now they sometimes went to the morning service with Mam but she didn't insist, and Clo had gradually lost interest, preferring to spend the morning curled up with a book instead. She found it hard to believe that God was interested in what went on in Rushworth anyway.

14

When she got in, Mam was sitting at the table reading the newspaper. She looked up, frowning.

'You're very late, Chloe, I'm afraid your tea's spoilt.'

She bustled into the kitchen to rescue Clo's chops from the oven.

'Don't worry, Mam, I like them well done.'

'Have you been practising all this time?'

'*Rehearsing*,' Clo corrected, 'yes, we were doing the last scene tonight—we're all in it and it's difficult sorting out where everybody's supposed to be.'

She tucked into a chop.

'Mam,' she said, between mouthfuls, 'what's that bit about doing things the very best you can or not bothering?'

'You mean in the Bible?'

'Mmm.'

Mam went over to the sideboard drawer and got out a well-thumbed Bible.

'Just a minute.' She licked her finger and riffled through the pages.

'Here it is, Ecclesiastes chapter 9: 'Whatever your hand finds to do, do it with all your might,' is that the one you mean?'

'Yes. Something Mr James said tonight.'

'Oh? What was he on about, then?'

'The play.'

Then, because she could never hide much from Mam, 'They thought I wasn't trying very hard. Miss Redmond said if I didn't feel up to it I could drop out, but if I stay then I've got to give it my best shot.'

'They're quite right,' Mam said, 'if a job's worth doing, it's worth doing well.'

'Yes, but I just can't seem to feel very keen on anything at the moment.'

'It's to be expected for a while, lovey, it's the shock. But you know we shan't think any the worse of you if you do give it up.'

'Oh no, I've said I'll do it,' Clo said hurriedly, 'I want to do it. I just need some inspiration!'

She pressed one hand dramatically to her forehead and gazed at the ceiling.

Mam laughed. 'All right, pet, it's up to you, but remember—"with all your might"—it doesn't matter if it's not much, so long as it's your best, that's what counts.'

She got up and fetched her coat.

'Now, will you be all right on your own for half an hour while I nip out to see Mrs Askins? She's got 'flu, she may need something fetching from the shop.'

'I'll be fine, I'll have the radio on for a bit and wash up.'

'Bless you. Eric may be back before me, anyhow. See you later.'

Clo turned on the radio to the opening music of 'The Archers: An Everyday Story of Country Folk'. She listened with half an ear as she swished the soap suds round the sink.

'Oooh Eddee!'

The voice of one of the characters caught her attention: Clarrie Grundy—a modern version of Shakespeare's Audrey, the simple country girl who took herself very seriously! Brilliant! Clo couldn't wait to find her script and try out all her lines in Clarrie Grundy's voice.

She was enjoying acting in front of the bedroom mirror when she heard the front door open and Eric and Mam come in together, talking excitedly.

She entered the living room to hear Eric say, 'Yes, they said she can definitely come home in a fortnight!'

He could only mean one person.

'What's that?' she begged. 'Is Beth coming home?'

'She is!' Eric grinned, 'Sister tipped me the wink tonight. They're giving us plenty of time to make arrangements.'

'What kind of arrangements?' Clo was puzzled.

'All sorts of things, lovey,' Mam said, 'I'll have to hand in my notice at work for a start, and we'll have to think how to get her up and down stairs.'

'But what...?'

Clo didn't understand. Why couldn't Beth walk upstairs like everybody else?

'She's very weak,' Eric explained, 'we'll have to get her around in a wheelchair for a bit. But hopefully she'll start to improve when she gets back to the things she's used to.'

'Oh,' said Clo, 'I see.'

Mam got the calendar down and began working out dates.

'Oh dear, it's your play in a fortnight too. She'll be home by then. That means we won't both be able to come.'

Clo's face fell.

'But don't worry, pet, if I come on the Thursday maybe Eric will be able to make the Friday, depends how she settles in. How's that? You know we wouldn't want to miss it.'

'Yes, that's fine,' Clo answered, but she was disappointed that Eric and Mam wouldn't be there together.

'Other people's parents will be there,' she thought. 'I know they haven't all got two but I haven't even got one parent, not around anyway. It's not fair.'

She became aware of a horrible sensation creeping up from her stomach, like fear, only it wasn't that. It was resentment. Resentment at Beth for not being better and for spoiling her acting debut.

3

Clo sat in the gym at a desk which served as a dressing table, squinting into the mirror. She wore a white peasant blouse, a black lace-up bodice and a stripy red and orange skirt with a little apron attached. Her hair was screwed up in ratty pigtails and she had been made up by Mrs Simms the French teacher.

'Goodness,' she thought, 'I look like I've escaped from *The Sound of Music*!'

On her feet she had a pair of real Lancashire clogs. They made her clump, which suited her character perfectly. Miss Redmond liked her Clarrie Grundy voice and Derek could hardly keep his face straight in their scenes. Clo had thrown herself into the play, she lived and breathed the part; she even caught herself talking like Audrey (or was it Clarrie?) in shops or on the bus. It helped her forget about Chloe Olerenshaw and *her* problems for a while. Tonight was the technical rehearsal and painfully slow, stopping every few minutes for lights to be adjusted or to move bits of scenery. Clo, who didn't appear until Act 3, had been sitting around for ages.

Jenny Hall, who played Rosalind, came in and flopped down next to her.

'Phew, I'm shattered!' she groaned, tugging off her cloak.

She was dressed as a man for the scenes where Rosalind disguises herself as Ganymede. Clo thought her too pretty to be convincing, like the principal boy in pantomime. 'How is it going?' she asked.

'Slow, but not too bad,' said Jenny. 'Bit boring for you, isn't it? At least I'm on stage most of the time.'

'Oh, I don't mind. I couldn't learn hundreds of lines anyway, I don't know how you remember them all.'

'Everybody says that but honestly it's not difficult. If you listen, all my lines are written like poetry, so it's easier to learn.'

Clo gazed at her admiringly. 'Hey, fancy that!' She thought for a moment. 'I don't think my lines are in poetry.'

'No,' said Jenny, 'they're not. Only Shakespeare's posh characters speak it. Peasants and funny people speak normally!'

Clo was impressed and thrilled to be having a literary discussion with the star of the show.

'By the way, Clo,' Jenny said, hesitantly, 'how's Beth? We haven't heard anything lately.'

Clo had been trying to put Beth out of her mind. 'Oh, she's coming out of hospital today. She's in a wheelchair because she can't walk or anything.'

'How awful! Poor Beth. Is she going to get better?'

'I expect so, it's what they call a Reversible Brain Injury. It's just a matter of time.'

Mr James appeared in the doorway. 'Rosalind and Celia on-stage for Act 3 Scene 2, please, we're going on.'

Jenny grabbed her cloak and ran off in the direction of the stage.

Eric came to meet Clo afterwards and as they walked home Clo told him about the rehearsal.

'When you're on-stage the lights are so bright you can't see the audience,' she said, 'it's like being in a separate world. And I've got a pair of red clogs to wear, just like that photo of Mam when she was little.'

'That's smashing, Clo, I'm glad you're enjoying yourself.' He waggled his left hand at her.

'Notice anything?'

'You've had your plaster off. Is it better?'

'Not bad, it's a bit stiff but it's knit OK, that's the main thing. I'm going to need both hands for our Beth.'

There, he had broken the spell. Everything else evaporated in an instant.

'Is she?...'

'Yes, we've got our little lass back home. The doctors have done all they can. It's up to us now.'

Clo felt like a sack of coal had just been heaped on her back.

When she got home the whole flat was disrupted as everything revolved round a limp, unresponsive Beth who didn't speak or move of her own accord, but just sat or lay where she was put.

'I don't know how I'm going to get her downstairs on my own,' Mam worried, 'it needs two with the wheelchair and everything.'

'Don't fret, Mabel,' Eric said, 'we'll find a way.'

In the end only Mam came to the play. Clo tried not to notice all the Good Luck cards and flowers on the other desks—Jenny had loads but of course she was the leading lady; Derek Gibson had sent her one and made her blush. But none for Clo.

'I'm sure Mam would have remembered if she hadn't been so busy,' she told herself.

On the other hand, the flat was overflowing with cards and flowers for Beth. Rushworth Methodist had sent a huge basket of golden chrysanthemums but Beth hardly seemed to notice them.

'They're wasted on her, really,' Clo thought.

Swallowing her disappointment, she resolved to give the audience their money's worth.

'You scared?' asked Mary Lewis, a Year 9, who was playing Phebe, another country wench with rather more lines than Clo.

'No, not really.'

'Lucky you, I'm petrified! Are your folks here?'

'I think so.'

Mam had been in a tizz at teatime. 'I've just realized, it's only a week to Christmas and I haven't done a thing!' she groaned, trying to coax Beth to eat and make a shopping list at the same time.

'My Mum and Dad and sister are all coming,' Mary went on, 'I wish they wouldn't. I'll probably forget my lines and they'll keep on and on about it for weeks. Dad used to be an actor, he has very high standards,' she explained, gloomily.

Once the play began it all happened in a great rush, and soon Clo was waiting in the wings with Derek. She remembered just in time to remove her glasses and slip them into the pocket of her skirt.

'No jewellery, watches or spectacles,' Miss Redmond had warned, 'unless they're genuine seventeenth century ones, of course!'

Clo could see just far enough to get across the stage without an accident. She felt so excited she could hardly wait to begin. Then the lights changed, there were a few bars of rustic music, Derek seized her hand and they were on!

When she spoke her first line the explosion of laughter which greeted her from that dark space beyond the footlights almost stopped her in her tracks—they liked her! She was making all these people laugh! She blinked in the strong light and they laughed again. Clo responded enthusiastically to their appreciation, she revelled in it. All too soon the

20

performance was over and she was lining up with everyone else to take a bow. The thunderous applause made her tingle with excitement. Clo was on cloud nine.

'Well done everybody,' Miss Redmond shouted over the hubbub in the gym. 'Good first night, but tomorrow— tomorrow I expect even greater things!'

Clo scrubbed at her face with tissues, struggled out of her costume, and found her glasses. She craned her neck to see over the crowd of parents and friends near the door. Yes! Mam was there, right at the back. Clo pushed her way through.

As she passed, a tall man was saying to Mary Lewis, 'Not bad at all, darling, I've got one or two notes for you. Now, your friend Chloe's a nice little actress and no mistake...'

Mam hugged her. 'Oh Clo, I'm that proud of you! I was a bit late but they let me in all right. You had me in stitches, lovey!'

Instead of going straight home, Mam steered Clo towards the town centre.

'Little treat,' she said, 'Eric said to take you for a slap-up supper. D'you fancy Macdonald's?'

Clo was ecstatic, 'Ooh yes! Oh Mam, thanks!'

Such things were usually reserved for birthdays; Clo felt pampered and important. She loved the bright lights in the restaurant and the crowds in the street outside. She wriggled with pleasure as she tucked into her supper.

Mam sat opposite in her best coat, smiling and sipping coffee.

'You did take your part well, Clo,' she said. 'I wish you'd had more to do, I do really, I could have watched you all night! You're like your mum.'

She gave a little sigh. Mam seldom mentioned her daughter Denise, who hadn't been back for years and was no letter-writer.

'She did all sorts when she was young, dancing, playing the piano. Always did a turn at Chapel concerts—a voice like an angel. I think you and Beth must have shared it out between you.'

She made it sound like Denise had died and left them her talents in her will.

Clo didn't know what to say; she felt awkward talking about a mother she could scarcely remember.

'I do like stories,' she reflected, 'even if they're only pretend. And I do like making people laugh.'

'That's a special gift to have,' Mam said. 'You're going to need it to make Beth laugh again, and probably the rest of us too, before we're through.'

Beth again! Just when Clo was riding on a wave of happiness. She looked down.

'It might not be easy for you, lovey. You know we've always tried to give you both equal attention but Bethy's going to need a bit extra until she's better.'

'Yes,' Clo said, her supper sticking in her throat.

She changed the subject. 'Were you sorry to leave The Homestead?'

Mam had finished work the previous week.

'Yes, I'm fond of the old dears, and of course we need the money, but some things are more important. I'm afraid Christmas will be a bit less than usual, Clo, try not to mind, eh?'

Clo felt a great surge of love for Mam and Eric.

'Oh, Mam,' she whispered, 'it doesn't matter, honestly, so long as we're all together, but...' she faltered, 'we... we will still have a Christmas tree, won't we?'

'Of course we will, lovey. If nothing else we shall certainly have a tree.'

Christmas wasn't a bit less, it was as much as ever, and more. Rushworth Methodist rallied round with gifts, fruit and a gigantic turkey, and the lights on the promised tree twinkled in the firelight.

'Look, Beth!' Clo cried as she added one well-loved bauble after another, 'isn't it beautiful? Shall we have the fairy or the star on top this year?'

The merest flicker passed over Beth's pale face as she lolled in her chair by the fire but she didn't answer, and after a while Clo stopped asking and just got on with it.

'It's like having a complete stranger in the house,' she thought, 'you never really know if she understands, she just stares at nothing half the time. I want the real Beth back.'

She lay awake at night listening to Beth's breathing and felt repulsed. It was like sharing a bedroom with someone she didn't know and couldn't escape. So much space was needed for the wheelchair that Clo ended up crammed into a corner with most of her books and belongings stowed under her bed. She had no privacy now, because Beth never went out. It was a relief when the holidays were over and she could go back to school.

The weeks dragged on. Beth didn't improve as quickly as everybody seemed to expect. Now there was no play to lose herself in, Clo had to face up to reality. She tried to apply herself to her neglected school work.

'I know I need to catch up,' she thought, despairingly, 'but it feels like I'm running on the spot and never getting anywhere. And Mam and Eric are completely taken up with Beth. They can't be bothered with me.'

She knew it was hard for them. Mam couldn't carry Beth downstairs on her own so she was stuck indoors most of the time. Only when Eric was home or Mr Thompson from Chapel came could they get Beth and the wheelchair downstairs. But then Mr and Mrs Kawalski from the bottom flat poked their heads out and tut-tutted at the noise; it was all very awkward.

Clo struggled at school and felt lonely and unhappy at home. The same grey, detached feeling she had experienced after the accident enveloped her again and she could take no pleasure in anything.

4

'Chloe Olerenshaw—my office, please, at break!'

Mrs Cooper, the Head-teacher, poked her head round the door of 2R, bringing Clo suddenly back to earth.

Lizzie Lewis, who sat next to her, made a 'Poor you!' face.

Oh dear, what was up? Probably her abysmal homework again.

'I can't understand it, Chloe,' Miss Redmond had said, only five minutes ago, as she returned her last essay, 'English is supposed to be your best subject. I thought you loved narrative poems, but you've hardly managed a page on the "Ancient Mariner" I'm afraid it's just not good enough. Do it again.'

'I do love poems that tell stories,' Clo thought, 'the longer the better, but I can't get interested. It's like... like the dead albatross round the neck of the Ancient Mariner—this great weight round my neck, so heavy I can hardly lift my head.'

When she reached Mrs Cooper's door Miss Redmond was there too.

'It's all right,' she said, 'you're not in any trouble, but I think we all need a little talk.'

Clo stared at her feet until the door opened.

'Sit down,' Mrs Cooper said briskly.

She came straight to the point: 'Chloe Olerenshaw, I'm extremely unhappy with your recent performance.'

Clo thought immediately of the school play, then realized that Mrs Cooper was referring to her school work.

'You're a bright girl, creative and intelligent, but everything you've produced in the last two months has been scrappy, careless and untidy. What have you to say for yourself?'

Clo picked her thumbnail.

'Well?'

'Sorry, Miss.'

'But why, Chloe, why?'

'I don't know, Miss. I've tried to catch up but I just can't. Beth—' She stopped.

'Beth?' Mrs Cooper prompted, her voice softer, 'what about her?'

Clo felt like a nasty whingeing kid, but it all tumbled out: 'Everything's for her now. I know she can't help it and I hate her being like she is, but it just takes up all the time and space... it fills everything.'

The two teachers looked at one another.

Mrs Cooper came round the desk. She touched Clo on the shoulder.

'I think I understand,' she said. 'When these tragedies occur they seem to throw everything else out of kilter. I suggest that, for a while, you spend games lessons in the library catching up with your work. I'm sorry, you may have to miss swimming too, but we can't have you falling behind at this rate. Do your best, Chloe.'

Outside, Miss Redmond said, 'I'll sort things out with the games staff for you. Do your homework at school for now. I expect there's plenty for you to do at home.'

'Yes, Miss.'

Lizzie was waiting for her in the yard. 'What happened, Clo?'

'Oh, I've just got to do some extra work to catch up.' Then she beat her chest with her fists and cried in a sorrowful voice, 'But it means missing games and swimming for weeks and weeks! How ever will I cope?'

Lizzie stared, then realized Clo was acting and laughed. 'Oh Clo, you lucky old thing! I wish I could stay in the warm instead of freezing on the hockey pitch!'

The following morning Clo was halfway out of the front door when Mam panted downstairs behind her.

'Clo!' she cried, 'it's Friday, you've forgotten your sports kit!'

'I don't need it.'

'Why not, pet, is it cancelled?'

'Er, no, I am!'

She explained. 'I'm not to do it for a while, I've got to catch up with my work—but I don't mind. You know me, I've never been the sporty one.'

Mam sat down heavily on the bottom stair. 'Have you been in trouble?'

'A bit,' Clo admitted, 'Mrs Cooper said I'd got to do better and I said it was a bit... difficult working at home just now, so she said I could do it at school when the others are doing games.'

Mam looked stricken. 'Oh, lovey, I'm sorry, I've been that

tied up it never occurred to me—it must be impossible. Forgive me?'

'Mam, don't, there's nothing to forgive, it's not your fault. I'm sorry, I'm not much help. I just don't know what to do.'

'We need to help each other, pet. Let's make a promise to try. From today, yes?'

'Yes!' Clo kissed her. 'But I must dash or I'll be late and then I'll get detention as well—see you tonight!'

Mam got up off the cold stair, rubbing her back, just in time to see Mrs Kawalski peeping disapprovingly through a chink in her door.

'Morning, Mrs K!' she called.

The door slammed shut. She sighed and made her way back upstairs to Beth.

Next day was Saturday and Eric was at work; somebody was off sick and it was an opportunity to do some overtime. With Mam giving up her job, things were a bit tight. This meant they were all stuck in the flat.

Trying to be helpful, Clo volunteered to do the shopping.

'It'll be a bit heavy for you, pet,' Mam said, 'are you sure?'

'I'll do it in two lots, I'll use your shopping trolley and you can help me carry it upstairs.'

'That sounds sensible,' Mam agreed.

She sat down at the living-room table to make a list. 'Now only get that sort of coffee or none at all, get a big packet of rice because it's cheaper than a small one, and have a look in the meat counter to see if there's anything we like reduced because it's near its sell-by date—use your common sense, lovey.'

On the way to the supermarket Clo stopped to have a look in Mr Rashid's Sari Shop. She loved the shimmery materials. She liked Mr Rashid too. Once, when she was nine, she had gone in and asked how much they cost. Mr Rashid was amused and gave her a plastic bag full of off-cuts for nothing. All Clo's dolls had brilliantly-coloured caftans and saris that year. Mr Rashid saw her and waved.

In Savemore's, she was unsure how to cope with a supermarket trolley as well as her own. As she hesitated she heard a thin laugh and turned to see who was making fun of her. There was no one but a smartly-dressed old lady with pink hair, sitting in a wheelchair.

'No need to struggle, my duckie, why don't you leave your trolley here with me? It'll be quite safe—I won't run away with it!'

'Oh thanks,' Clo said, 'that would be a help—I won't be long.'

'Take your time. My daughter will be ages, I can see her gabbing nineteen to the dozen down the other end of the store. I don't mind, I enjoy sitting here watching the world go by.'

Clo set off round the store. It wasn't as easy as she'd expected; the wheels on her trolley didn't want to go the right way so she kept banging into other people.

'Like being on the dodgems at the fair!' she thought.

The aisles were so long she missed the signs and had to keep retracing her steps to find what she wanted. Just when she was getting really fed up she heard a voice behind her.

'Hi, Clo, have you lost something?'

It was Mary and Lizzie Lewis.

'I can't find the stupid rice anywhere!' she wailed in mock despair, 'I'm sure I've seen it once.'

'It's with the pasta,' Mary said, 'come on, I'll show you. Aren't you used to Savemore's?'

'I haven't done it on my own before, it's so confusing.'

Mary agreed. 'Lizzie and me have been doing it for a while, we've got a new baby and he takes up all Mum's time. What we do is go up and down all the aisles the whole length of the store, that way we don't miss anything and it's quite fun really—ah! here's the rice, what sort do you want?'

Clo consulted her list. 'Short-grain, large, it says here, thanks. Right, meat next.'

'Want me to come?'

Clo didn't want them to know that she was going to buy reduced meat and said hurriedly, 'No, thanks—got to learn to do these things on my own! See you.'

'We'll wait for you at the checkout,' said Lizzie, 'we can walk home with you.'

Clo found some half-price mince and joined a queue for the till, where she had a brief panic that she might not have enough money.

'Phew, just made it!' she said to the woman on the checkout, whose badge said her name was Lillian.

'Well done,' said Lillian, handing her the receipt and two pence change.

Clo's shopping was now sitting in a heap at the end of the checkout.

'Need a carrier?' Lillian was on to her next customer and saw the danger of a pile-up.

'Er, no, I've got a shopping trolley somewhere,' Clo said, looking round.

She saw the old lady waving to her and ran to collect it.

'Thanks.'

'A pleasure, duckie, at least I can still be of some use to somebody.'

Clo wondered how she could be so cheerful stuck in a wheelchair.

The Lewis girls were waiting for her outside. Clo dragged the heavy trolley behind her.

Lizzie said, 'Here, let me help, I've got a free hand.'

She took hold of the other end of the handle and pulled alongside Clo.

'You look like a pair of donkeys pulling a cart!' laughed Mary.

Clo and Lizzie hee-hawed and giggled along the pavement.

'Let's go through the park,' Mary suggested, 'before you trample somebody to death!'

They dawdled happily along the gravel paths. Spring bulbs were beginning to poke through the soil and the bare trees were getting a green haze on them.

'You made a big hit with our Dad when you were in the play,' said Mary.

'Oh, really?' Clo was pleased.

'Yes, he was so impressed with you he just went on and on about your performance instead of picking mine to pieces!'

'Oh dear, does he do that?'

'He can't help it, having been a professional actor and all that, nothing would be good enough, but he's very nice really, he doesn't mean to be horrid.'

'What does he do now—for a job, I mean?' Clo asked.

'You'll never believe it,' giggled Lizzie, 'but he's a vicar!'

'Well, a minister,' said Mary. 'He went back to college—he must have been the oldest student ever—and he starts ministering this week.'

'It's a bit different to being an actor,' reflected Clo.

'Oh, I don't know,' Mary said, 'Mum says it's surprisingly similar. But just think of us, Clo, it's bad enough having an actor for a Dad, but a minister! Just think how good and holy everyone will expect us to be—it could be a great strain!'

She shrieked with merriment and the other two joined in, putting on angelic expressions then laughing helplessly at one another.

Lizzie and Mary lived further on, in Chorley Fields, so they parted at the end of Raglan Street. Clo arrived home still giggling. She hadn't laughed so much for ages, she felt as if she'd just had a double dose of vitamins.

She pushed open the front door and shouted, 'Mam, I'm back!' then clapped her hand over her mouth in case Mrs Kawalski came out and complained.

Mam bustled downstairs. 'Well done lovey, however did you manage everything?'

'Mary and Lizzie Lewis were there. They showed me where everything was and we had a real laugh on the way back!'

'That's nice,' said Mam, 'It's done you good, you've got a bit of colour in your cheeks. You can go shopping again!'

'Yes, I will,' Clo said. 'And Mam, an old lady in a wheelchair looked after the trolley for me.'

'Did she have a pink rinse and glasses?'

'Yes.'

'That will be Mrs Wilkins from Stanley Street. She's crippled with arthritis but she still takes an interest in everything. Next time you see her tell her you're Mabel Appleby's granddaughter, don't forget.'

In the afternoon Mam asked Clo to stay with Beth so she could pop out to do the flowers at Chapel for a special service next day. The new, helpful Clo agreed. She switched on the TV for Beth and burrowed into the sofa with a book. She was totally absorbed in *Watership Down* when she heard an odd noise. Looking up, she realized that the noise was coming from Beth. She jumped up, appalled. What was wrong with her? Then she noticed the television. Being Saturday afternoon it was all sport and just at that moment the gymnastics were on. Beth was obviously upset and was crying in a rusty, creaky sort of way.

Clo switched off immediately. She found a hankie up her sleeve and began to dab awkwardly at Beth's face. At that moment the door opened and Mam came in.

'Now what's going on here?' she demanded, snatching the handkerchief from Clo.

'There, there, my pet, what's the matter? Tell Mam all about it!' she soothed, wiping Beth's nose as if she were three years old.

She looked up at Clo. 'Well?'

Clo took a step backwards. 'She... she was watching the sport on telly,' she faltered, 'the gymnastics came on and she started crying. I'm sorry, I was reading.'

Mam's face changed. 'Oh, was that it?' she said. 'I see. Well, you can't really be blamed for that. Pop the kettle on, pet, and we'll all have a cuppa.'

A few seconds later she came into the kitchen.

'I'm sorry I flew at you, Clo,' she said, 'I thought... well, I don't know what I thought, but it's good in a way. It was obviously the gymnastics did it, it upset her to see something she used to be so good at. It proves she's noticing things, but I think we'd better be careful what she sees in future, we don't want to distress her when she's so weak.'

When they went back into the living room Beth was her usual lifeless self, almost as if nothing had happened.

'I'd like to take Beth with me to Chapel in the morning,' Mam said, as they were drinking their tea. 'We've got a new minister starting tomorrow—that's why we were doing a special job on the flowers. I'd be really pleased if you'd come too, Clo, I could do with an extra pair of hands.'

Privately Clo thought she'd rather have a lie-in with her book but, remembering her promise, she said, 'OK, Mam, I'll come.'

5

Spring sunshine brightened the dingy pavements of Raglan Street. Eric carried the wheelchair downstairs and Clo stood guard whilst he and Mam went back for Beth. As she waited the door to the bottom flat opened and Mr and Mrs Kawalski emerged, dressed head to toe in shiny black.

'Good morning!' Eric called cheerfully, edging downstairs with Beth in his arms while Mam hovered behind with a large tartan rug. 'Lovely morning!'

'Maybe, maybe,' admitted Mr K stiffly.

Mrs K sniffed and followed him out.

'If they ever smile,' muttered Clo, 'their faces will crack.'

Beth was wrapped up tightly in the rug. Clo had on her red duffel coat and an orange, yellow and green stripy woollen hat which she had bought at the school jumble sale.

'Oh, Clo, you can't wear that for Chapel,' Mam protested.

'But Mam, my ears stick out under my beret,' Clo pleaded.

'Oh... all right, I haven't got time to argue, but you take it off before we go inside, all right?'

'OK, Mam.' Clo patted her favourite hat happily.

At last they were ready. Eric waved them off then made his way round the back to their tiny bit of garden for his Sunday morning potter.

As they approached Waterloo Road they were greeted by two of Mam's friends, also on their way to Chapel.

'Morning, Mrs Appleby, glad you could make it.'

'Morning, Mrs Allsopp,' Mam said, 'well, it is a special service, after all...'

'Morning, Mabel,' the other woman broke in, 'I hear you've left The Homestead, then?' Clo remembered Mrs Thorne—she always liked to know what was going on.

Mam replied, 'Yes, Agnes, I had to, it would have been too difficult with Beth at home.'

'I know they'll miss you, Mabel, you're so good with the old folk. My Auntie Annie can't praise you highly enough.'

Her eyes fastened on Clo who was trying to be invisible behind the wheelchair.

31

'And how nice to see you again, Chloe, I hear you've become quite the little actress. But you're going to have to be Granny's little helper now, aren't you, and help look after poor dear Elisabeth—what a tragedy!'

She raised her eyes heavenwards and even Mam winced.

'But,' she finished brightly, 'these things are sent to try us!'

When they reached the Chapel door they stopped, wondering how to get Beth up the steps.

Albert Thompson, who was one of the stewards, hurried over to help.

'Next week,' he said, 'we'll get that wooden ramp out the basement, that'll make life easier for you. Now ladies, where would you like to sit? I think you'll find there's more room for the chair down at the front and you'll get a good view of our new minister.'

'Oh no,' thought Clo, 'why do we have to sit at the front where everyone can see us?'

'You wheel Beth down,' Mam said, 'I'll get the hymn-books.'

Clo was left with her sister. She gave the chair a tentative shove and found it moved quite smoothly. Self-consciously she began to push.

Mrs Allsopp murmured, 'What a good girl!' as she passed.

She was relieved when they reached the bottom of the aisle and she could hide in the pew. When the first hymn was announced Mam, who had brought three hymn books, found the place and put one on Beth's knee so she could see it. Clo thought this unnecessary and was sure everybody was looking at them. In fact they were all on their feet, and halfway through the first verse. She suddenly became aware of what they were singing:

> Now thank we all our God,
> With hearts, and hands, and voices;
> Who wondrous things hath done...

To Clo the words seemed singularly inappropriate but she liked singing. She stood up and joined in.

The Reverend Howard Lewis was introduced.

'I'm so pleased to be here,' he began.

Clo's ears pricked up; she couldn't see him because Mam was in the way but surely she had heard that voice somewhere before? It was when he mentioned his theatrical background that Clo recognized him.

'This must be Lizzie and Mary's dad,' she thought excitedly, 'the one who used to be an actor!'

She had never imagined he would turn out to be the new minister of Rushworth Methodist Church! She shuffled along the pew to get a better view.

'What's up?' Mam hissed.

Clo whispered, 'Mr Lewis—he's Mary and Lizzie's father!'

After that she hung on every word he said. After all, he had once called her 'a nice little actress'.

'Being a minister,' he said, 'is exactly the opposite of what you might think. I'm not here to tell you what to do, I'm here to serve you, that's what ministry means. We must all learn to serve one another in love, and love has to be unselfish, generous—extravagant, even, without expecting to get anything back. The way God loves us.'

He chuckled.

'It's a bit like acting on television, really—you put your all into it during the filming but you never really know if anybody will bother to switch on and watch when it's finished!'

Clo was riveted by this. She remembered the laughter and applause when she'd been Audrey in the play, how satisfying it was, how warm it had made her feel. During the prayers that followed she opened one eye and scanned the church. The Lewis girls were in the front row of the balcony, sitting with a dark-haired woman wearing a beautiful blue jacket, who was trying to keep a wriggling baby still.

'Their Mum and baby brother,' she thought.

The girls had their heads down, but Mrs Lewis was more concerned with the baby, who began to cry. She gathered him up in his shawl and edged out of the row towards the exit door.

Then all at once the service was over. Clo waved frantically until Mary noticed and waved back, leaning over the balcony so dangerously that Albert Thompson called, 'Now you watch it, young Mary, or you'll be over the edge!'

Everyone queued up to shake Mr Lewis's hand. Albert went to the front and tapped the microphone.

'Ahem! May I remind you good people that there's a nice cup of tea waiting for you downstairs in the hall—you can meet Mr Lewis and his family down there.'

The crowd thinned magically and Clo and Mam were able to get Beth's chair up the aisle.

Mr Lewis shook Mam's hand. 'Mrs Appleby,' he beamed, 'I'm told that you are responsible for the exquisite flower arrangements. Thank you so much.'

'It's my pleasure, Minister.' Mam almost dropped him a curtsey.

'And these are... ?'

'My grandchildren,' Mam said, 'Chloe, known as Clo and Elisabeth, known as Beth.'

Mr Lewis's eyes gleamed mischievously. 'Oh no, I think you're mistaken,' he said, pointing at Clo, 'this one is definitely called Audrey—or is it Clarrie Grundy?'

They laughed. Clo was surprised he'd recognized her without her costume and said so.

'Oh, I couldn't forget that super little cameo performance,' he said. 'Hello again, Clo, love the hat!'

Mam shot Clo a look.

'And nice to meet you, Beth. I have an Elizabeth as well— oh but you must know the girls already?'

'Yes,' said Clo, 'Lizzie sits next to me in class and Mary was in the play.'

'Excellent. Now, why don't you all come down to the hall for a cup of tea?'

'We-ell, I'm not sure if that's practical...' Mam began.

'Beth's chair?' he asked. 'No problem. I'm sure the valiant Albert and one of his henchmen—sorry, it's henchpeople these days, isn't it—will help. Albert! Here a minute...'

He disappeared.

Mam was astonished by Mr Lewis's flamboyant manner. 'He's certainly different!' she remarked, 'not like old Mr Theobold at all.'

'It's because he used to be an actor,' Clo said.

'And,' she thought, 'he liked my hat so he must be all right!'

Down in the church hall Clo and the Lewis girls relocated one another.

'Fancy seeing you here!' said Lizzie. 'Didn't know you came to church.'

'I don't really,' Clo said, 'at least, I'm not sure. Mam asked me to come to help with Beth.'

'What did you think of our Dad then?' asked Mary.

Clo grinned and struck a pose. 'I think it was a super little cameo performance,' she pronounced.

'Wha-at?' Mary gasped.

'Well, that's what he said about me!' said Clo, and they laughed so hard people began to stare at them over their teacups.

Mary said primly, 'Behave, Lizzie, remember we're the minister's daughters and we're supposed to set an example!' and they were off again.

'What are you up to?' asked a voice.

Clo recognized the sky-blue jacket of Mrs Lewis; she was fascinated to see that it was Chinese with a lovely swirly dragon on the back.

'Mum, this is Chloe Olerenshaw,' said Lizzie. 'She was in the play, remember?'

'Of course she was,' said Mrs Lewis, 'nice to meet you, Chloe.'

'And this is our baby,' said Mary jiggling the pushchair with her foot, 'he's called Joel.'

'Joel?'

'Yes, after the prophet!' chimed the two girls in unison.

Clo didn't understand the joke.

Ginny Lewis rolled up her eyes. 'Stop it, you two, hundreds of people are called Joel. He's an old chap in the Bible, Chloe, and do *you* think my innocent babe looks like an ancient prophet?'

'When he screws up his face to howl he looks about a hundred!' said Mr Lewis, joining them.

'Mmm, yes,' said his wife, 'I must train him only to do that during the hymns. I had to remove him during prayers, I didn't think his contribution would be appreciated.'

Clo liked Mr and Mrs Lewis, they had a quirky sense of humour. You were never quite sure if they were being serious or having you on.

'Must circulate,' said Mr Lewis. 'Come to tea some time, Clo.'

'I'll send word,' said Mrs Lewis. 'Bye.'

Clo almost danced home.

'It was definitely a good idea bringing you this morning,' Mam said. 'Fancy your friends being there. Perhaps you'd like to come again some time?'

'Yes,' said Clo, 'I probably would.' She had a feeling that Chapel was going to be a whole lot livelier since the Lewises had arrived.

A couple of days later she sat in the school library staring out of the window.

'It might almost be worth doing games to be out there in the sunshine,' she thought.

A sudden 'Pst!' in her ear made her jump. Lizzie Lewis, still in her games kit, thrust an envelope into her hand.

'It's a note from Mum to your granny,' she told her, 'asking you to tea on Friday.'

'Smashing!' said Clo. 'Thanks.'

'You can walk home with me,' Lizzie said, 'I'll show you where we live.'

'I'm dying to see it. Having a real house and a proper garden must be fantastic.'

'We shan't be there much longer, we're moving to the Manse, the house that belongs to the church, as soon as it's been done up.'

Clo was crestfallen. 'How can you bear to leave Chorley Fields?'

She had only seen it from the bus but she knew that it was very different to Waterloo Road.

'Oh, we're looking forward to living nearer town and the shops and everything,' Lizzie said.

'Quiet, please, in the library!' Mr James interrupted them. 'Elizabeth Lewis, what are you doing in here? This is not the hockey field—scram!'

Lizzie scuttled out and Clo tackled her French with new enthusiasm.

Mam pounced as she was leaving for school on Friday: 'Let me look at you, have you got a clean blouse on? And let me see your shoes... Mmm, they could do with a polish if you're having tea with the minister.'

'Oh, Mam!' cried Clo, 'Lizzie and Mary won't have put a clean blouse on specially and anyway, Mr Lewis won't be there.'

'You'll do as I say, Chloe Olerenshaw!' retorted Mam. 'You're not going to show me up. Now hurry, the ambulance will be here in a minute.'

Beth had begun to attend the hospital once a week to see a psychologist and a physiotherapist. Mam liked to make the most of this and squeeze in as many jobs as possible.

Clo gave her shoes a quick flick with the duster, and pelted downstairs to avoid any further inspection.

Fifteen, Sycamore Avenue was not as grand as Clo had

imagined, but it did have wrought-iron gates and a cherry tree in the front garden and that was good enough. Ginny Lewis opened the front door before they reached it.

'Welcome to the madhouse, Chloe!' she called. 'Come in, make yourself at home, I'm just getting the baby up.'

She wore an ankle-length embroidered skirt, sandals and a baggy T-shirt with 'This is a Nuclear-Free Zone' printed on it. Her long black hair had escaped from a purple hair-band down her back.

'I wonder if she's a hippie?' thought Clo.

Lizzie led the way to the kitchen and Mrs Lewis soon reappeared, with a sleepy Joel grizzling over her shoulder.

'He didn't want to get up,' she explained, 'and who can blame him? Why come out into the cold world when you've got a nice warm cot? Do you like babies, Clo?'

'Er, I'm not sure...'

'I wouldn't blame you if you didn't,'—Mrs Lewis looked sternly at her small son—'horrid, whingeing little things, always demanding attention. I prefer them when they're older—about twelve.'

Lizzie said, 'Oh, Mum!' in a horrified voice.

'Take no notice, Chloe!' laughed Mrs Lewis. 'We're all a bit mad in this house—of course I love him to bits, but babies are very time-consuming and not always very good company. Lizzie my love, amuse your little brother while I make tea.'

She bustled about the kitchen throwing things into pans while Lizzie bounced Joel on her knee. Clo timidly offered him a finger. He grasped it and chuckled toothlessly.

Tea was spaghetti followed by cream cakes. Mam would never have called it a 'good tea' but Clo thought it delightful. Mrs Lewis spooned mashed banana into Joel, most of which ended up on the floor.

'In real life, I'm an artist, I illustrate books,' she told Clo. 'I've got my hands full at the moment, as you see, but when we move I'm hoping to get back to work—along with all the other little duties expected of a minister's wife!' She made a comic face.

'She really is a most unusual mother,' thought Clo. 'I think she's great!'

When Eric came to collect Clo, Mrs Lewis said, 'I've been thinking, Mr Appleby, it will be Easter soon and Mary, my eldest, will be away on a geography field trip. D'you think we could borrow Clo for a few days to keep Lizzie company?'

Eric, still boggling at Mrs Lewis' appearance, recollected himself enough to answer, 'That's very kind of you, Missus. It'd be a nice change for her, we've been that took up with her sister...'

'Yes, of course you have, so maybe it would be a bit of a breather all round?' suggested Mrs Lewis. 'How would you like that, girls?'

'Smashing, Mum!' Lizzie hugged her.

'Oh, thank you, thank you!' cried Clo, clapping her hands, 'I'd like it more than anything else in the whole world!'

6

Things were looking up for Clo; she still spent games lessons in the library but gradually this began to pay off; Miss Redmond was all smiles as her essays improved.

'Mustn't make too rapid progress though,' she joked to Lizzie, 'or it will be back to the dreaded sports field for me!'

Beth's progress was slower. She responded now with the odd yes or no, but to Clo she remained a stranger, wearing Beth's clothes and sleeping in Beth's bed. Not that she cared so much, now she had Lizzie and Mary for her friends. They went to Savemore's on Saturdays and sat together in Chapel on Sundays.

The first morning of the Easter holidays Clo woke with the delicious knowledge that she was about to escape to Chorley Fields. She squinted at the sleeping Beth and hugged herself with pleasure.

'I won't be here tonight,' she thought, 'hooray!'

She jumped out of bed and dressed quickly.

'By heck, you're the early bird!' exclaimed Eric, who was enjoying his first cup of tea. 'See this, Mabel,' he called to Mam, 'this lass can't wait to run away to Chorley Fields!'

Clo felt guilty because it was true. She couldn't wait to leave the crowded little flat for the large, exciting Lewis household.

'Only joking!' Eric said. 'It's nice you can have a little holiday, we may not get a real one this year. Just don't forget us, eh?'

'Forget us!' scoffed Mam, 'she's only going for a week! Now Chloe, I hope you'll be a credit to us.'

'Of course I will—they're all crazy there anyway!'

Mam was shocked. 'You mustn't talk about the minister's family that way. I admit they are a little... unusual, but I expect they'll change when they move to the Manse.'

'I do hope not!' Clo thought.

Ginny Lewis and the girls arrived at 9 a.m. Mam stared: Mrs Lewis was wearing a pair of tight red leggings with black stars on them and a very baggy sweater; her hair was tied up on top of her head, straggling down all round like an untidy nest, and she bounced into the shabby living-room like an exotic bird. Clo couldn't help comparing her with Mam in her big pinny, her sensible shoes and not a hair out of place.

'Oh, if only Mam were like Mrs Lewis!' she thought.

But then, of course, she wouldn't have been Mam. She gave her an extra hug. She was halfway out of the door when Mam called her back.

'Have you said goodbye to Beth, Clo?'

'Er, no, I think she's asleep.'

Mam gave her a look.

Clo ran through to the bedroom, stuck her head round the door and called, 'Bye Beth, see you!' then made a dash for freedom.

They rattled down Raglan Street in Mrs Lewis's battered green Morris.

'Right,' said Ginny, as soon as they'd waved Mary off on the coach for her field trip, 'let's take advantage of this unaccustomed freedom and go contemplate a little interior decor!'

'What she means is,' Lizzie translated, coldly, 'Daddy's looking after Joel and she wants to poke round the Manse.'

They drew up in front of a large dilapidated house near the church, and Clo jumped out to open the creaky gates so they could drive through. Ginny fished around in her handbag for a bunch of keys and tried several before hitting on the right one. The heavy oak front door had a little sunset made of coloured glass set into it.

Lizzie lagged behind, kicking up gravel on the drive.

'C'mon child!' her mother yelled. 'Don't you want to see your new home?'

No response.

'What's the matter, Lizzie?' Mrs Lewis peered into her daughter's sulky face.

Lizzie looked sternly at her. 'Honestly, Mum, you do go over the top sometimes! What on earth must Clo's family think of you, dressed like an old hippie?'

'Hey, less of the old!' her mother ordered. 'Am I an embarrassment to you, my poor child? Did I really shock them, Clo? I was late this morning, I just threw on the nearest clothes and dashed out, I'm afraid.'

'I think Mam was a bit surprised,' Clo said. 'You're different to most of the people we know. But if you're the minister's wife she'll think whatever you do is OK. I think you look super, I love your leggings!'

Ginny grinned. 'Why, thank you, Clo, you have very good taste. By the way, where's your wonderful hat?'

'I couldn't find it this morning, I think Mam might have hidden it.'

'Just think how boring life would be if we were all the same.' Ginny led the way through the hall into an old-fashioned kitchen. 'Goodness, look at this! It must have been auctioned off from the Ark!'

Even Lizzie giggled and they began opening cupboard doors and poking around in the pantry, frightening wood-lice and spiders.

'How on earth did the old minister live in this dump?' Lizzie asked.

Clo knew. 'Mam says he didn't, it got too much for him; he had a room at Mrs Thorne's until he retired.'

'That accounts for a lot,' Ginny said, tearing down cobwebs to open the back door. 'Oh look, smashing garden. Go and explore while I take some measurements.'

They waded through waist-high grass. Daffodils and tulips were struggling to see above the overgrown borders and a couple of apple-trees, badly in need of pruning, were exploding into leaf. At the bottom of the garden was a stone bench rather like a chapel pew.

'Oh, it's wonderful,' cried Lizzie, balancing on the back of the bench, 'but I expect it will all have to be tidied up, and guess who'll be recruited for the job? It'll take ages to tame this jungle!'

Clo mimed a pair of binoculars. 'Goodness knows how many wild animals are lurking in the undergrowth, you could advertise safaris! Oh Lizzie, I do like your Mum, she's so...'

'Weird?' Lizzie suggested.

'No, unusual and—creative—yes, that's it, creative.'

'She's certainly that!' agreed Lizzie. 'I don't know, I just worry what people think of her sometimes. She's got some pretty odd friends too, from when she was at Art School—they make Daddy look almost normal!'

'I think you're lucky to have such interesting parents,' Clo said. 'I think you're lucky to have parents at all.'

There was an awkward silence.

Then Lizzie said, 'Didn't you ever know your mum and dad, Clo? Did they die when you were little?'

Clo searched her memory.

'I don't remember my father, he went away when we were

41

tiny, but I can just remember Mum. She's not dead, she's a singer—sort of musicals and clubs—we were always moving around so she could be in shows. When we had to go to school it got difficult because we were never in one place long enough. In the end Mam came to get us and we've lived with her and Eric ever since.'

'Does she ever write to you or phone you up, your mum?' asked Lizzie.

'Only birthday cards sometimes. The postmark on the last one was Chicago! They wrote and told her about Beth ages ago but she hasn't answered. She's probably moved on somewhere else by now.'

Lizzie chewed her pony-tail and thought that it was probably better to have strange but residential parents than none at all.

Ginny came crashing down the garden. 'OK, girls, I've measured up, we must go and rescue Daddy. We can come again soon.'

As they entered the front door at Sycamore Avenue they heard a plaintive voice crying, 'Help! Help!'

Ginny merely raised an eyebrow and went into the kitchen while Clo and Lizzie dashed into the lounge.

Mr Lewis was lying on the hearth-rug pretending to wrestle with Joel who gurgled delightedly.

'Ah, help at last!' he gasped, 'save me from this delinquent baby!'

Laughing, Lizzie took Joel and Mr Lewis jumped up and ran for the door, wild-eyed and gasping, 'Coffee, coffee, give me coffee!'

Clo watched in amazement. 'Is he always like that?' she asked.

'Quite a bit,' Lizzie told her. 'I tell you, it can be very tiring living with two comedians!'

Clo thought it would be great fun.

Mr Lewis hugged his coffee cup and grinned round the kitchen at them all.

'Nice to have you with us, Clo. Now, you have a choice: you can either sleep in the spare bed in Lizzie's room or you can have Mary's—assuming it is possible to find it beneath all the junk.'

'Mary's room, please,' Clo answered immediately.

Lizzie looked hurt. 'Oh,' she said, 'I thought you'd want to share with me.'

Mr Lewis said, 'Lizzie, you and Mary are very lucky to have a bedroom each. I'm sure it will be a change for Clo to have some personal space, am I right, Clo?'

Clo nodded.

'You'll be together all day, anyway, you'll probably want a rest from each other at night.'

Lizzie brightened and Clo was relieved that she hadn't upset her friend.

Ginny asked them to sort out the garden shed for moving, and they had a wonderful time poking round in boxes and filling bin-bags with rubbish.

'Oh, what's this?' Clo cried, opening an old shoebox. It contained lots of newspaper-cuttings, photographs and theatre programmes.

Lizzie peered inside. 'I think it must be Dad's old theatre stuff, we mustn't throw those out—they're family history.'

She lowered her voice. 'Can you keep a secret, Clo? Only you mustn't tell, or Dad might be banned from preaching.'

Clo stared at her. 'Of course I won't tell. What is it?'

'Well,' Lizzie whispered in Clo's ear, 'he once appeared on telly, in "Coronation Street!" '

'No! Really, truly? What did he play?'

'Sshh!! A con-man. So you can understand why nobody must know.'

At that moment the guilty party entered the shed.

'What a load of junk!' he exclaimed, 'I think a bonfire is called for, don't you?'

'Yes, yes!' cried Lizzie, jumping up.

'Be careful not to burn these, Mr Lewis,' Clo said, handing him the box.

'Well, I'll be... my murky past skulking in this innocent-looking shoebox. Maybe it ought to be consigned to the flames? Much the safest!'

'Lizzie told me about "Coronation Street", but don't worry,' Clo assured him, 'your secret is safe with me.'

Howard Lewis looked puzzled. 'Oh, that. It's no secret, Clo, half of Britain saw it!'

'But Dad, you said they mustn't know at church,' Lizzie protested.

Mr Lewis bellowed with laughter. 'I was joking, darling! How could it be a secret, really?'

Lizzie was cross. 'I thought you were serious—I should have known you were just being silly!' She scowled at him.

'Sorry, sweetheart,' her father said, 'I *was* being silly but it's not the sort of thing you go round telling everyone. It might look like I was showing off and that, my dearest daughter, is most unbecoming in a Man of the Cloth! Forgive me?'

'OK, but as a penance I think you should make us a barbecue as well as a bonfire.'

'Good idea,' said her father. 'Er, did you by any chance notice the equipment during your excavations?'

A rusty old barbecue with one leg missing was unearthed and Mr Lewis took charge of it. Clo and Lizzie piled up rubbish and garden debris for the fire while Ginny cheered them on. Then she disappeared into the house and returned with a box of fairy lights.

'My contribution,' she announced.

She draped them over the shed and plugged them into an extension lead.

'We'll have to wait till dark for the proper effect,' she said. 'I'll go and dig something vaguely edible out of the freezer.'

Clo couldn't wait till nightfall. She'd never been to a barbecue—people didn't have them in Raglan Street.

By 6.30 she and Lizzie were tending the crackling bonfire. Mr Lewis happily reduced sausages and beefburgers to lumps of charcoal on the barbecue. The fairy lights twinkled and the stars came out. Clo couldn't remember seeing anything more beautiful in her life, or tasting anything nicer than the blackened burgers. Ginny kept running inside for more bits and pieces to chuck on the fire. Lizzie and Mr Lewis seemed astonished at this.

'Look, don't stop me,' she laughed, 'enjoy it, you're always complaining about me hoarding things!'

'My wife,' Mr Lewis explained to Clo, 'should have been a squirrel!'

All too soon they ran out of things to keep the fire going, the last burnt offering was swallowed, and the barbecue itself burnt through and collapsed.

'It was already on its last legs,' quipped Mr Lewis and the others groaned.

Half an hour later Clo and Lizzie sat on Lizzie's bed dunking ginger biscuits into scalding cocoa.

'I wish I could stay here for ever,' said Clo, 'I've never had so much fun in my life. Except for the play.'

'I wish you could too, but wouldn't you miss your gran and Eric and Beth?' Lizzie asked.

'I suppose so. It's just that your family's so interesting.'

'And I sometimes wish they were less interesting!' said Lizzie. 'Perhaps we could arrange a swap every so often?'

'Brilliant idea!' yawned Clo, 'Gosh, I'm tired, see you tomorrow.'

'Me too,' said Lizzie climbing under the bedclothes, "night, Clo.'

Clo went into Mary's room and shut the door. What a day! And what luxury to have a whole room to herself. She went to the window. The fairy lights were still on in the garden, twinkling through the branches of the trees. She looked up and saw the stars twinkling back. 'Oh, thank you,' she said to Whoever had provided all this, 'I'm so happy.'

Next morning Ginny said, 'We'll deliver Lizzie to her piano lesson and go and have another look at the Wreck, shall we, Clo?'

'What wreck?'

'The Manse. That's how I've thought of it ever since we saw it the other day.'

Clo giggled.

'We'll have Jo in tow so we can't do much, but you can give me some advice on colour schemes.'

She was hauling washing out of the tumble drier.

'Botheration!' she cried, holding up a shrunken pair of red leggings. 'Oh well, they were only cheapies off the market, into the duster drawer with them. Unless... I don't suppose you'd fancy them, would you, Clo? I know my two wouldn't be seen dead in them!'

'Yes, please!'

Clo almost snatched them from Ginny's hand and tore upstairs. They fitted perfectly and she danced down in them.

'Very fetching!' said Mr Lewis, emerging from his study. 'Much more suitable on you than on a minister's wife!'

His wife aimed a swipe at him. 'Goodness knows what your granny will say.'

Clo smiled sweetly at her. 'I'm sure you'll talk her round! Thank you, Mrs Lewis, I just love them.'

Lizzie shook her head. 'I don't know which of you's worse!' she said.

When they got to the Wreck Ginny said, 'Let's have a look upstairs, I'd like my studio right at the top.'

They entered a huge attic room with windows facing onto the garden.

'Now, Clo, in your opinion, what colour should I paint this room?'

Clo considered. 'Well, I think you're going to want all the light you can get if you're going to work in here. I think it'll have to be... white?'

'Absolutely right,' Ginny said, 'anything else would change the colour of what I'm working on.'

'I wanted to paint our bedroom at home orange,' Clo told her, 'but the others thought it would be awful and we had pale yellow in the end.'

'Mmm yes, orange could be a bit overpowering in a small room,' Ginny said.

'Yes, it is small, even smaller now...'

'But in a huge room like the lounge downstairs it could look absolutely stunning. Let's go, Clo!'

Downstairs Ginny surveyed the lounge.

'Oh yes! It will look wonderful—the sun floods this room in the afternoons. Not a fierce orange though, more a warm gold. This room will be golden! Isn't that right Jo-Jo?'

She jiggled Joel up and down until he chuckled in agreement.

In the garden Ginny exclaimed delightedly as she discovered the flowers and plants half-hidden in the grass.

'Look at these hyacinths, don't they smell heavenly?... and narcissi and jonquils—oh lovely... and do you know, I believe there's an early orange blossom down by the wall?'

She parted the apple branches.

'Come and smell this—it's gorgeous!' she called.

She buried her face in the creamy blossom. 'Oh Lord, you made lots of lovely smells, but this one really takes the biscuit!'

Clo was amazed to hear her talk to God as if he were one of the family. She pushed through with Joel in her arms and sniffed the delicious scent; her throat felt tight with the beauty of it. 'Mmm, it's heavenly. How I wish...'

'What do you wish?'

Clo spoke yearningly into the baby's wispy hair, 'I wish I was going to live here and that Beth was back and... well, that everything was different.'

'Oh dear,' Ginny said, 'don't spoil the pleasure of the moment with "if onlys". Life is never plain sailing, I'm afraid, but God keeps us going with delightful little presents, like this.'

She touched the blossom.

'And this,' taking Joel from her.

'And this,' pointing at the sun.

Clo thought of the fairy lights and the stars the previous evening.

'Enjoy them, Clo. Who knows what might be round the corner? But worry about that when it comes, and enjoy the present, eh?'

Clo looked up at Ginny, her face framed by the orange blossom, her hair all over the place and the baby dribbling happily down her jumper.

'Yes, I'll try,' she said, 'I'll really try.'

The first words Mam uttered when they walked through the front door were, 'Chloe Olerenshaw, what *have* you got on!' She was staring at the red leggings, of course.

'Aren't they lovely?' Clo said. 'Ginny—I mean Mrs Lewis— gave them to me.'

Mam was confused because Mrs Lewis was there, wearing an equally stunning purple pair.

'I see,' she said, 'well, if Mrs Lewis thinks they're suitable...'

'I hope you don't mind, Mrs Appleby, I shrunk them in the wash and I thought Clo could muck about in them and save her other clothes.'

Good old Ginny!

'Very sensible,' said Mam, 'thank you very much, Mrs Lewis. I hope she's been a good girl.'

'Why,' thought Clo, 'do adults talk as if you weren't there?'

'She's been a great help,' Ginny assured Mam. 'She's kept Lizzie company, given me some decorating advice and I think she's even getting used to babies! I hope you'll let her come and stay again?'

'That's very nice of you, Mrs Lewis,' Mam replied, though she didn't answer the question.

7

Exams were looming but Clo now felt confident enough to face them. Mrs Cooper said she could start doing games again, but she begged to be allowed to continue in the library. It was still hard to study at home.

Beth's friend Jenny stopped her in the corridor one afternoon.

'Clo,' she said, 'you know it's the Swimming Gala in a couple of weeks? Well, Miss Poole was wondering whether Beth would like to come. She says we could pick her up in the school bus and bring her home afterwards. The Gala wouldn't be the same without her.'

Beth had been Junior Champion the last two years.

'You could ask Mam,' Clo said. 'I'm sure she'd enjoy it, she always loved the Gala.'

'Will it be OK if I call in after school this afternoon?'

'Yes, sure, do you know where we live?'

'Vaguely, but give me the address again. I'm a miserable toad for not coming before. I suppose I've been a bit, well, scared to,' Jenny admitted.

Clo wrote their address on the back of Jenny's jotter.

'I know what you mean,' she said, 'but there's no need. She still doesn't talk much but she knows what's going on. She doesn't see many people so it would be great if you came round.'

As soon as Clo got home she knew something was wrong because Jenny was standing in the kitchen, looking worried, and Mam was in the other room with Beth who was crying noisily. 'What's up?' she whispered.

Jenny whispered back, 'Not a good idea after all, I'm afraid.'

It seemed Beth had shown real pleasure at seeing her friend, but when Jenny had suggested the Swimming Gala Mam had immediately said, 'Oh no, Jenny, I don't think that would be a good idea at all, she'd find it very upsetting.'

Beth had appeared to bear this out by bursting into tears and banging her fists on the arms of her chair.

Mam came through, closing the door behind her.

'It was a nice thought, Jenny love, but not a very wise one. You see how it's affected her? It's terrible for her to be reminded of what she's lost. But you mustn't blame yourself, and please thank Miss Poole.'

'That's OK,' Jenny said, 'I didn't mean to upset her. Can I come again some time and bring Janice?'

'Yes, come again,' Mam said, 'but please be careful not to talk about anything that might upset her.'

'We'll be really careful, I promise.'

During this conversation, Clo had been listening to Beth. She couldn't help feeling that her crying sounded more like frustration than despair.

Clo told Ginny what had happened.

'Your granny is a very loving lady,' Ginny said, 'but I do think perhaps she's being a bit over-protective. We all have to learn to cope with things we can't do for one reason or another. But it's not for me to interfere, Clo, things are hard enough for your Mam as it is. Maybe we'll think of something, eh?'

Clo nodded.

'I see you're still wearing your leggings!' Ginny chuckled.

'Yes, they're my favourite things. Mam's never mentioned them again.'

Mam didn't seem to notice what she wore these days. She and Eric spent most of their time making lists and doing sums. They talked for hours, in low voices, long after Beth and Clo were in bed. Nothing was said but Clo got the impression that they were pretty hard up.

Exams were nearly over, only English to go. The night before, Clo was over at the Lewises, revising. At 8 p.m. Ginny came in with cocoa and chocolate biscuits.

'Time to rest your brains, ladies,' she announced.

She sank comfortably into a sag bag.

'How goes it?'

'Pretty well,' Lizzie answered. 'It'll all be over tomorrow, then only a fortnight to the holidays, whoopee!'

'That's what I want to talk to you about,' Ginny said. 'Clo, you know we're moving very soon? There's loads to do so we're packing the girls off to the seaside to Youth Camp for a fortnight. We wondered if you'd like to go with them.'

'Go on, Clo,' urged Lizzie, 'it's really good fun, we go most years and meet lots of people we know, it would be great to have you along!'

'Oh, I'd love to,' Clo said, 'but I don't think we could afford anything like that.'

'Don't worry,' Ginny reassured her, 'there are ways and means. Tell you what, Howard can ferry you home tonight and have a word, howsabout that?'

'Ye-e-s!' Lizzie and Clo shouted together.

Clo was almost bursting with excitement by the time they reached Raglan Street.

Mr Lewis said, 'Now stay cool, Chloe! Let me do the talking and we'll get it all sorted, OK?' She beamed at him.

As they went in they could hear Eric arguing with someone on the phone. Mam hurried through to the living-room, fussing and smoothing her hair when she saw Mr Lewis.

'May I have a word, Mrs Appleby?' he said. 'Or is this the wrong time?'

'No, no, it's all right, Minister, please sit down,' she said, pulling the door shut on Eric and hovering nervously.

Clo had a horrible feeling that she had come home in the middle of another crisis. If Mr Lewis felt it too he didn't let on.

'Mrs Appleby,' he began, 'you must know how much we all enjoy Chloe's company. Our younger daughter, Elizabeth, in particular values her friendship.'

'Oh yes, yes, thank you, that's nice to know,' Mam fluttered.

'We've arranged to send the girls to the Methodist Youth Camp at Brinkley, they've been several times before and love it. Mary's older now and prefers friends her own age, so it would be really nice for Lizzie if you'd allow Clo to come along and keep her company. What do you think?'

Eric entered the room. He looked worried.

Mam glanced at him and took a deep breath. 'It's very kind of you, Minister, we're very grateful for all the interest you've shown in Chloe and I'm sure Youth Camp is splendid for them but I'm afraid we just couldn't manage...'

Mr Lewis interrupted, 'You mustn't worry about the expense, I assure you the church has the resources to sponsor any of its young people who might benefit from a couple of weeks at Camp. There's no question of a charge.'

Clo looked round triumphantly but, to her horror, Mam sat down heavily at the table and covered her face with her hands.

Eric squeezed her shoulder. 'It's not as simple as that, I'm afraid,' he said.

'Would you like to tell me what the problem is?' suggested Mr Lewis, kindly. 'After all, it's what I'm here for.'

Mam looked up gratefully. 'Thanks Minister, we could do with some guidance, things are really getting on top of us. The neighbours have made a complaint about Beth's chair and the noise. Eric was just trying to reason with them—was it any good, love?'

''Fraid not, Mabel, we're going to have to find another way.'

Clo was up in arms. 'Mr and Mrs Kawalski, you mean? Why, the mean, stuck-up pigs, they hate everybody!'

'That's enough!' Mam was angry. 'They've had a hard life. You don't know what dreadful things happened to them in the War. Don't ever let me hear you speak like that again!'

'Chloe, you've got an exam tomorrow,' said Mr Lewis, 'why don't you get ready for bed and I'll try to sort a few things with your granny and Eric, OK?'

'OK. Sorry, Mam. Night, Eric, night, Mr Lewis.'

'Night night, lovey,' Mam said, 'I'll come and tuck you in later.'

Clo lay in bed in the dark and prayed, 'Oh God, if you're listening, please, *please* let it be all right for me to go to Brinkley with Lizzie and please make the Kawalskis nicer, Amen.'

She was sound asleep when Mam looked in an hour later.

'Well?' whispered Lizzie next morning as Clo slid into her desk for the exam.

'They haven't said,' Clo whispered back, 'did your dad say anything?'

Lizzie shook her head. 'Nope!'

Miss Redmond rapped the desk for silence and began to give out the papers.

'Good luck!'

'Same to you.'

Clo spent the first few minutes gazing out of the window, thinking about last night. Then she caught sight of Miss Redmond. Her expression clearly said, 'Get on with it Chloe, what are you wasting time for?'

She put everything else out of her mind and concentrated on the paper. Her eyes lit up when she saw an extract from the 'Ancient Mariner'. She was still writing when Miss Redmond stopped them.

'Goodness, have you written a book?' asked Lizzie.

'Quiet, Elizabeth, examination rules apply until all the papers are in!' called Miss Redmond. 'As that was your last examination, this afternoon you will have extra Games— Chloe, you may join in with the tennis class. I'm afraid you have no excuses now!'

To her surprise Clo quite enjoyed bashing a ball around in the sunshine, and the rest of the school day passed quickly. Immediately the last bell rang she made a dash for home.

She found Eric watching TV with Beth, and Mam bustling about in the kitchen.

'Hi, everybody!' she greeted them, striking a pose in the doorway.

Nobody smiled. Everything was unnaturally subdued.

Mam just said evenly, 'Hello Chloe, sit down and I'll bring you a cup of tea.'

She never called her Chloe unless she was cross or had something serious to say.

'What is it, what's the matter?'

Eric got up and switched off the TV.

'Sit down, lass,' he said, 'we need to talk about, well, things.'

Clo felt a block of ice form in her chest.

Mam stirred her tea for too long and looked worried.

Eric coughed. 'Clo love, we, us, as a family, have got to face up to one or two things—oh, nothing new, but things have come to a head, as you might say, and we've got to find a way through them. Do you understand?'

Clo remembered Ginny, surrounded by orange blossom, saying, 'You never know what may be round the corner...'

She held her breath and said in a tight voice, 'Yes. Go on.'

'Well...' Mam and Eric both began together and Mam said, 'Go on, love,' and Eric began again.

'As you must have realized, things haven't been very easy lately, money-wise. Since Mabel stopped working we've had nothing to spare so I've been doing all the overtime going. As a result I haven't been at home much and Mabel's had no help.'

'Because I've not been here either,' Clo thought, guiltily.

As if he had read her thoughts Eric said, 'We're not blaming you, Clo, we're dead pleased you've got friendly with some nice little lasses, but it has meant your Mam's been stuck. On top of it all, there's this problem about disturbing the Kawalskis, which is nobody's fault, but the thing is, they've complained to the landlord and, well, he's asked us to look for alternative accommodation—he wants us to leave.'

Clo was shocked. This was her home, she'd lived here almost as long as she could remember! She was speechless.

Mam leaned over and took Beth's white hand in her own chunky red one.

'And our Beth is still nowhere near right. We're going to have to face up to the possibility that she may not be able to do much for quite a while.'

Then, with a supreme effort, she added, 'maybe never.'

There. It was said. The block of ice shifted to Clo's stomach and she felt cold all over. What, never? Surely Mam didn't believe that? Even Eric seemed shaken that she'd actually said it. As for Beth herself, she turned her head away and said nothing.

'But if that's how it's to be,' Mam said staunchly, 'we must just pray that the Lord will give us strength to cope...'

She stopped and pressed her lips together very hard.

Clo rapidly went over all this in her mind: One, they were short of money; two, they had to find somewhere else to live, and three, Mam had admitted that she wasn't certain of Beth's recovery. Somehow she knew there was more to come. She was right.

Eric said, 'The upshot of it is, Clo love, much as we'd like you to go to Camp with your friends, it's just not possible— oh, I know it wouldn't cost anything but money's not the problem.'

'What then?'

'We've got to start house-hunting straight away,' he explained, 'but our present income won't be enough, rents have gone up that much. So Mabel's going back to The Homestead—they're still short-handed.'

Clo's mind raced. 'But who'll look after Beth... ?'

She knew the answer almost before the words were out of her mouth.

'Oh! Me?'

'That's right,' Mam said, 'I shall go back part-time when you break up. That way we should be able to make ends meet. So I'm sorry, lovey, we'll need you here for Beth while I'm out for a few hours every day—you're a big girl now, you're quite capable of helping.'

Clo thought she would stop breathing, she couldn't believe this was happening! Lack of money she could cope with, moving she could get used to, but to be stuck with Beth day after day for the whole holidays! Those lines from the 'Ancient Mariner' came back to her, they had been in her exam today—

> Instead of the cross the Albatross
> Around my neck was hung.

That was how it had felt before—like a dead weight round her neck. And the unlucky albatross was Beth! She stood up, trembling. She knew they were waiting for her to say, 'Yes, of course I'll do anything you want.' But she couldn't, she wouldn't.

'No!' she shouted, 'it's not fair! Just when I've got the chance of going on holiday with my friends—for free—I'm to be stuck with her! I'll have nobody to play with and nobody to talk to. Why can't you send her back to hospital? Why should I have to suffer? I hate you!'

She was crying now and backing away from them, feeling for the door handle. They were all staring at her. She opened the door and ran downstairs, not caring how much noise she made, out of the front door and away. She wasn't sure where she was going, she just wanted to escape. When she reached the end of Raglan Street she looked back but nobody was following her. After a second's thought, she began to run with all her might towards Chorley Fields.

8

Howard Lewis was preparing what seemed to him a rather clever sermon when the door bell rang—and rang.

'Answer it, will you, Mary?' he called.

Mary boggled at the dishevelled apparition on the doorstep.

'Please... can I see your mum? I can't... they won't...' Clo dissolved into tears.

Mary yelled, 'Mum, Dad, quick!'

Howard threw down his pen and strode into the hall. Ginny appeared at the top of the stairs with Joel screaming in her arms.

Howard took control: 'Don't panic!' He took Clo by the arm and propelled her into his study where he sat her in an armchair and handed her a box of tissues. 'Blow!' he ordered.

Clo took off her spectacles and blew her nose loudly. Howard perched on the edge of his desk and waited. She hesitated; now she was here her guilt and resentment seemed too unpleasant to confess. She gulped.

'I... Mam... they say I can't go to Camp because we're moving and Mam's going back to work and Beth's got to be minded and it's all Mr and Mrs Kawalski's fault and I feel...' —the tears started to flow again—'I feel—horrid!'

Howard suppressed a wry smile. 'That sounds like a pretty good assessment of the situation,' he said.

Then Clo remembered. 'But of course, you know already, don't you? You were there!'

'Yes,' he admitted, 'Mabel and Eric did talk it over with me last night. I'm really sorry about Camp, Clo.'

'Why didn't you tell them it was OK for me to go?' she demanded, 'they'd have listened to you!'

'Because it obviously wasn't OK, in the circumstances. Besides, I was only there as an observer, as you might say; they had to decide the best course of action for the whole family.'

They were all against her! Clo's sense of injustice and rage erupted; she stamped her feet and clenched her fists.

'It's not fair! It's not, it's not!'

Then her anger fizzled out and she dropped back, exhausted.

'Life, my dear Clo, on the whole, is *not* fair,' Mr Lewis observed quietly.

Ginny crept in with a tray of tea. She knelt beside Clo's chair and put her arm round her; she smelled of gripe water and talcum powder.

'Rough, eh?' she said sympathetically.

Clo buried her face in her old sweater and howled again.

Ginny let her cry herself out, then she mopped up the tears and put a mug in Clo's hand.

Hiccupping, Clo gulped the hot tea. Looking up she saw Howard and Ginny were smiling. She was confused: were they making fun of her?

Howard said, 'Good-oh, we've got some of that anger out, at least. Better out than in.'

'That's good?' Clo was surprised.

'Oh yes. If you hide it, it festers away inside and that's much worse.'

Clo said bitterly, 'I even *prayed* to go but God didn't answer.'

'Mmm, yes, difficult one that,' Howard reflected. 'The thing is, what you want is not necessarily, in the long run, good for everybody else. Your family need you very much at the moment, and I know it seems rotten, but God hasn't just got your welfare to consider, he's got Mam and Eric and Beth to think about too. I believe God *does* answer our prayers—it's just that sometimes he says No.'

Ginny said, 'I think he's got something more important for you to do than go to the seaside. It will certainly be more demanding, but doing things for other people *is* more difficult than doing your own thing. Though I've found it's often more rewarding.'

'But what if it's something I don't know how to do, I just *can't* do?' Clo pleaded.

'Can't! What's can't?' demanded Howard. 'It's amazing what you can do if you try. I'm not pretending it will be easy, but you won't be poor-little-Clo-all-alone, you know. We'll support you as much as we can and there will be others—you're not expected to shoulder the whole thing, nobody expects that.'

'Mam's always going on about carrying our burdens,' Clo sniffed.

'I think she means responsibilities rather than dead weights, and I bet she also talks about being helped to carry them. God helps us, if we let him. Oh, I know what you're going to say, is God going to shove this wheelchair round Rushworth all day long? No, of course he isn't. Amazingly, God relies on us to do those sort of things for him, but he helps us so it's him anyway... sorry, I'm not explaining it awfully well, am I?'

Ginny laughed. 'He's not been doing this for very long, Clo!'

Clo couldn't help smiling.

At that point the telephone rang.

Howard picked it up saying, 'I bet I know who this is—ah, hello, Mrs Appleby! Yes, yes, don't worry, she is here. Yes, I think she'll live... don't worry, we'll bring her home... no, no trouble at all, all part of the service! Bye now.'

He replaced the receiver.

'Is she very cross?' Clo asked.

'No, just worried because you'd gone out without your coat!'

'I was really horrid to them before I left.'

'I don't think she'd given that a second thought. She was more worried whether you were safe. But if you were horrible, why don't you say sorry?'

'Yes, I will,' said Clo, humbly.

Ginny jumped up. 'Right, time for tea. Hungry, Clo? Because if not you'll just have to sit and watch us all stuffing ourselves before I take you home.'

Clo realized that she was ravenous. 'Oh, yes please, I'm starving!'

'I'm not surprised,' Ginny said, 'nothing like a bit of drama to stimulate the appetite.'

'Shall we have a little prayer first?' Howard suggested.

'Good idea,' agreed his wife.

Clo wasn't sure. Praying in church was one thing, her own hurried requests last thing at night another. This was a bit too serious, too *involving*. But Howard prayed very simply, talking to God as though he were a trusted friend, asking him to help her in the weeks to come. She felt strangely comforted as they went through to the kitchen.

'Gosh, Clo, what's up?' said Lizzie, 'your eyes are all red!'

Ginny answered for her. 'Clo's got a lot on her hands at the moment, girls, but she's going to be OK , we're going to cheer her on and, at this particular moment in time, feed her!' She began dishing out an unidentifiable casserole with baked potatoes.

Lizzie said, 'Does this mean you can't come with us to Brinkley?'

Clo nodded, her mouth full.

'Oh rats! I'm really sorry. Never mind, it's only for two weeks and we'll send you postcards, lots. Will you write to me?'

'Sure!' That, at least, was something to look forward to.

Ginny drove her home.

'Want me to come in?' she asked.

'Yes. No!'

'Which?'

'No. I've got to sort it out by myself. But thanks so much for... everything.'

Then, on impulse, she said, 'I do love you!' and threw her arms round Ginny's neck.

'And I love you too, Chloe Olerenshaw,' said Ginny, hugging her back, 'lots of people do. Don't forget—it may not be easy but we'll help you all we can, OK?'

'OK!'

Clo watched the Morris disappear round the corner, took a deep breath and rang the bell.

Mam cried and forgave her, and Eric patted her and said, 'Good lass!'

Beth just mumbled, 'That's all right,' without looking up and continued to stare fixedly at a newspaper until Mam wheeled her off to bed.

Later Mam, Eric and Clo sat down together and began to work out some practical details for the summer. When she finally crawled into bed Clo felt several years older than she had been at teatime. Now she must begin to take responsibility, ready or not.

'It's a bit like jumping in the swimming baths at the deep end,' she thought, 'when you're not even sure you can swim.'

On the last day of term Clo was alone in the classroom clearing out her desk when Miss Redmond came in. She was relaxed and cheerful, anticipating the final bell and six weeks holiday.

'Well, Chloe, are you pleased with your examination results?'

Clo had done well, particularly in English and Art where she had gained 'A's.

She nodded. 'Yes thank you, Miss.'

'You did very well to catch up,' Miss Redmond said, 'and between you, me and the gatepost, I'd be surprised if you didn't get a prize next Speech Day.'

'Really?'

'Yes. We like to encourage pupils who maintain a good standard under difficult circumstances.'

Miss Redmond made herself comfortable on Lizzie's desk.

'I understand you've got your hands pretty full for the holidays?'

'Yes, rather, I'm helping look after Beth while Mam goes back to work.'

'So I hear. How do you feel about it?'

'I don't know,' Clo admitted. 'I've started to help; I know how to fold up the wheelchair and put it together again and how to help Beth in and out of it. She can walk a bit now so I don't have to lift her. I've got to take her out whenever the weather's nice and wheel her around. It will be pretty boring.'

'Oh, it needn't be boring!' Miss Redmond exclaimed. 'There's lots to see in the neighbourhood. You could go in a different direction each day and explore—more interesting for both of you. Then there's the library and the parks... is she beginning to show more interest in things now?'

'It's hard to say, she watches the telly and she talks a bit if you ask her things. She's better than she was.'

'That's good,' said Miss Redmond. 'It's important to keep talking to her. You see, she will suddenly begin to improve and then there will be no stopping her.'

Clo hoped it would happen before the holidays finished.

'Yes, Miss, I expect so.'

Miss Redmond stood up. 'I'll be hiking in Turkey for the next few weeks but after that, if I can help in any way, my number's in the book. I'm the only D. Redmond listed.'

'Thanks, Miss, that's really nice of you.' Clo tried to imagine her elegant English teacher legging it through Turkey with a rucksack.

'Don't forget,' said Miss Redmond.

As soon as she had gone Lizzie bounced in. 'Hi! I saw Miss R and ducked out of sight. Everything all right?'

'Yes, fine. I was just mucking out my desk. Hey, you'll never guess!'

'What?'

'Miss Redmond is going hiking in Turkey for the holidays! Can you imagine it?'

'Goodness, do you think she'll go in her high heels?' said Lizzie and they dissolved into giggles.

'Are you coming round tonight?' Lizzie asked when she had recovered. 'We're off on Monday and I won't see you for at least a fortnight.'

'Come home with me, I'll ask Mam,' Clo said. 'I think she'll say yes. After all, it's my last weekend of freedom. She'll be at work next week and then I'm doomed.'

She made a tragic face.

Lizzie put her arm round her. 'I know,' she sympathized, 'hard luck.'

That night Clo really did feel as though she had been sentenced to six weeks' hard labour. She sat on Lizzie's bed watching her stuff assorted clothing into her suitcase and sat on top while Lizzie locked it. She felt torn: half of her knew that her help in the next few weeks was vital and that people thought she was grown-up enough to do it properly; the other half was just desperate to go on holiday and do silly, fun things like everybody else. She clutched a chocolate wrapper bearing Lizzie's address for the next two weeks and a tear trickled down her nose landing smack in the middle of the paper, smudging the ink.

'Oh Clo!' cried Lizzie, hugging her, 'it really is too awful for you! It's not fair!'

'Sometimes it's OK, other times I think it's horrible. I'm all mixed up.'

'Yes, Daddy says it's often difficult to do the right thing but it's important to get on and do it, however you feel. Then it's supposed to get easier.' She sounded doubtful.

'I expect he's right.'

'Anyway, we'll be back soon and then I'll be able to help you.'

'Will you?'

'Course, we're best friends, aren't we?'

'Oh, yes, of course we are!' exclaimed Clo, gratefully.

For that moment, things didn't seem too bad at all.

9

On Sunday night the weather broke spectacularly with thunder, lightning and teeming rain. Clo lay watching streaks of light flare across the bedroom ceiling.

'Goodness,' she thought, 'I wonder if it's like this in Brinkley? I'm glad I'm not sleeping in a tent tonight—poor old Lizzie!'

At breakfast Mam said, 'You can't go out, the whole street is awash, you'll just have to amuse yourselves till I get back at 3 o'clock. Clo, help Beth get washed and dressed. There's some corned beef in the fridge for your lunch.'

'All right, Mam.'

Secretly Clo was glad that she didn't have to take Beth out today. With any luck she could spend the whole day reading. She helped her sister to the bathroom. Not sure what she was supposed to do, she soaped her flannel for her; Beth took it and wiped it slowly over her face, water trickling down her neck. Clo hovered for a moment, then grabbed a towel and put it round her sister's shoulders to catch the dribbles; Beth dropped the flannel and dabbed her face with the towel. She did everything in maddening slow motion. Clo squeezed toothpaste onto Beth's toothbrush for her. When she had finished cleaning her own teeth Beth was still staring at it.

'Shall I help?'

Beth shook her head and slowly began to clean her teeth. Clo felt a mixture of irritation and embarrassment. When she had finished Beth sat back limply on the loo seat, eyes closed, as though the simple task had exhausted her.

In their bedroom Clo inquired brightly, 'What do you want to wear? Jeans? Sweatshirt?'

'Not bothered,' Beth said wearily.

Clo rifled through the wardrobe. 'I know! What about your pink T-shirt dress?'

She had always admired the lovely rosy colour and the big, bold flowers printed on the front of the dress. She lived in hope of inheriting it.

Beth nodded. 'Yes, that one.'

Clo helped her into it.

'I'll lend you my pink scrunchy hairband to go with it,' she offered, then stopped dead as she realized Beth's hair was now much too short.

Their eyes met in the dressing-table mirror. Clo wanted to kick herself.

Beth said, 'Never mind,' and sighed.

Clo left her staring in the mirror while she dressed herself in red dungarees, sky-blue T-shirt and the trainers she had painted with acrylics last summer. Her feet had grown and they pinched a bit but she loved them too much to give them up.

They went through to the living room. It was still only 9.30. What should they do now?

'I'll put the telly on, shall I?' she suggested.

She positioned Beth in front of the TV. Then she found her book and burrowed into the sofa where she lost herself in *The Hobbit* for the rest of the morning. When Mam came home the two girls had hardly moved; Clo was finishing her book and Beth staring at a wildlife programme.

'Better in than out today...'

Mam took her umbrella through to the sink.

'Good gracious, what are you wearing, Beth? That's a best dress, not for wearing round the house—Clo, whatever made you put that dress on her?'

Clo shrugged. 'She wanted it.'

Mam frowned. It was obvious she thought vibrant pink wholly unsuitable for an invalid.

'All right, lovey,' she said, 'you wear it if it makes you happy. Now Clo, I hope you haven't just had TV on all day?'

'Er...'

'And I hope you were watching what came on.'

'Er... no, yes.'

Oh dear, minding Beth was going to be even worse if Mam was going to cross-examine her every day!

Mam seemed satisfied. 'That's all right then. Whew, there was plenty to do when I got back today! Old Mrs Goldstein's had another stroke but we're doing what we can for her and Mr Bradshaw wandered off again...'

She was obviously pleased to be back in the thick of things.

'... and the forecast's good for tomorrow, so you'll be able to go out. Mr Thompson will be round at 10.30.'

Albert arrived on the dot and carried Beth and the chair downstairs. Even though it was warm, she was tightly cocooned in the tartan rug—Mam's orders.

'She's not strong, she might catch cold,' she insisted.

Clo was comfortable in T-shirt and shorts and glad it wasn't her sweltering under all that wool.

'All right, pet?' Albert asked.

Clo nodded.

'It'll stay dry,' he said, confidently, 'I'm off to my allotment, the weeds will be growing like billy-oh after all that rain!'

He hopped on his bicycle and cycled off with a wave.

'Well, here goes,' thought Clo, 'I'm really on my own now.'

The morning streets were quiet and she managed to steer Beth around shoppers and other obstacles. A workman moved a warning cone so they could get past some road-works. Clo thanked him and he touched his cap and grinned. In fact most people were helpful as she negotiated kerbs and pedestrian crossings for the first time.

They stopped to look in the Sari Shop, Clo's favourite. Mr Rashid saw her over the back of the window display and waved. Then he saw the girl in the wheelchair. He turned and beckoned to his wife. Clo saw them point and shake their heads sadly at one another. She moved off quickly before they could come out to speak to her.

'We'll go to the park,' she said.

As they entered the big iron gates she remembered how she and Lizzie and Mary had giggled and skipped through them the day they'd met at the supermarket.

'I bet they're having fun at Camp,' she thought wistfully.

She positioned Beth's chair beside a bench in the sun. Beth seemed to enjoy the change of scenery and pushed back the heavy rug. A butterfly landed briefly on her arm and she said, 'Ahh!'

Clo settled down to read. She was deeply involved in her book when she became aware of a shadow across her feet. She looked up to see a grubby little boy of about six solemnly staring at Beth, who was dozing.

'Wot's up wi'er?' the child demanded.

Clo ignored him.

'Hey, I asked you,' he persisted, 'wot's the matter wi'er?'

Clo scowled. 'She's not very well.'

'Can't she walk?'

'A bit.'

'She's one of them spazzos, in't she?'

Clo was ruffled. 'No, she's not!' she retorted, waking Beth who blinked and mumbled something.

'She is, she is!' the child shrieked. He ran a short way across the grass shouting, 'Come over 'ere and see this spastic kid in a wheelchair!'

To Clo's horror he returned with three more scruffy little kids who lined up two metres away from Clo and Beth and stared.

'Go away!' said Clo, fiercely.

But they stood their ground and began to chant, 'Spazzo, crippo, spazzo, crippo!'

Beth closed her eyes again but Clo grew more and more furious. It was like being tormented by a pack of little yapping dogs. She was ready to lash out at them when two women pushing buggies appeared, smoking and laughing. One of them noticed the children; she tossed her cigarette into the nearest flower-bed and charged.

'Hey!' she yelled. 'What d'you think you're doing, you little beggars? Leave that off at once!'

She swiped the nearest child hard round the head, which set him howling and scattered the rest.

'Little animals!' she growled.

She turned to Clo who was close to tears. 'Sorry about that, pet, kids are dead cruel sometimes. They didn't mean no harm, don't you let 'em upset you.'

Her friend had caught up and an elderly couple with a poodle stopped to watch. Clo felt like a sideshow; for once she didn't like having an audience. She couldn't say a word, she was so humiliated. She stuffed her book in her bag and practically kicked the wheelchair into motion. Beth moaned in protest at the sudden movement but Clo took no notice; she put her head down and didn't stop until they were back in the High Street. She only slowed down as they approached the Oxfam Shop.

Now Clo dearly loved a good charity shop where she might find books and all sorts of bits and pieces; this prospect made her feel better. She began to manoeuvre Beth through the doorway.

'No! no! I'm sorry, you can't bring that in here!' called a shrill voice.

A tall, immaculately permed lady, with jewelled spectacles on a gold chain, bore down on them.

'It's all right, the door's wide enough,' Clo assured her.

'No, I'm *sorry*, there isn't room, it would be a fire hazard!'

Clo sighed. Defeated! A rummage in the Oxfam Shop would have cheered her up no end. She began to back awkwardly out of the door.

The bespectacled lady came closer. 'Why, it's Chloe Olerenshaw, isn't it?'

'Yes?'

'I remember you from *As You Like It*—I am Janice Fisher's mother.'

'Oh?' Clo wasn't surprised to hear it, Janice was bossy too.

Mrs Fisher lowered her voice to a loud whisper, 'And this is your unfortunate sister Elisabeth, am I correct?'

'Yes.'

'And I'm her unfortunate sister Clo,' she added silently.

'What a tragedy,' breathed Mrs Fisher, 'what a talented girl she was. How perfectly dreadful for you all.'

'Oh, we're managing.'

'Look dear, I'm sorry I can't let you bring her in but if you want to leave her outside while you look round, I'm sure she'll be all right.'

'OK.'

Clo went back inside but the pleasure had gone. Out of the corner of her eye she could see Mrs Fisher pointing and telling the other assistants about the 'tragedy'. After only a few minutes she slunk out from behind the dress stands.

'Don't feel like it today,' she said, 'let's go home.'

Wednesday wasn't much better. Clo discovered that there weren't many places you could take a wheelchair at all. Shops were too cluttered or had narrow doors or steps, and she didn't fancy the park again, too many kids. Where could they go? Miss Redmond had said that there were lots of interesting places to explore. Well, Waterloo Road stretched a long way into the distance; it might be worth seeing where it led.

After fifteen minutes or so they found themselves in an area called Brickfields which was new to Clo. There was a small street market selling fruit and veg and cut-price clothing and they looked round the stalls for a while. The smell from a hot-dog stall made Clo's mouth water; it must be lunchtime. There was nowhere to sit except a low wall at the edge of the market where a group of old men with shopping bags were discussing their purchases in a foreign language. They nodded politely and made room for her and Beth. Clo bought some crisps and they ate their lunch among the spoiled fruit and broken boxes. It was dirty and smelly, not the kind of place you'd want to stay for very long. Soon the market began to pack up and a dustcart hooted them out of the way. Clo began to push back the way they had come.

'I know, we'll call at the Wreck,' she said, 'maybe Ginny will be there.'

Beth agreed. 'Yes, all right.'

As they passed the church Mrs Thorne emerged, her arms full of cleaning materials. Too late, she'd seen them! Clo wished they'd gone another way.

'Dear children!' Mrs Thorne trilled, 'bless your little hearts! What a good girl you are, Chloe, looking after your poor sister while Granny is at work. Hello, Elisabeth!'

She waggled her fingers in Beth's face as if she were a baby in a pram. Beth's response was to close her eyes tight and pretend to be asleep.

'Oh dear,' Mrs Thorne said, 'she's not getting any better, is she? Poor lamb.'

Clo was rather cross with Beth because up until then she had been quite alert. Now she was playing the helpless invalid.

'... but the Lord giveth and the Lord taketh away, my dears, we must all bear our burdens. I took care of Auntie Annie until I couldn't manage any longer but now she's in your granny's capable hands. I can't tell you how happy she is that Mabel's back at The Homestead. Well, must run, bye-bye and God bless.'

She bustled off waving her tin of polish.

Clo thought, 'It's funny the way things work out. Mrs Thorne's got rid of Auntie Annie who is now being looked after by Mam so I have to look after Beth... you might call it Pass the Burden.'

'Hah!' She laughed mirthlessly and Beth opened her eyes and turned her head enquiringly, wondering what the joke was.

Clo couldn't tell her.

She trudged on towards the Wreck. Too late, Ginny was packing buckets, brushes and baby into the car as they arrived.

'Hi, girls!' she called. 'Bad timing, I'm afraid, I'm just knocking off for the day. How's things?'

'Oh, OK,' replied Clo, disappointed.

'I see,' Ginny said. 'Listen, why don't you both drop by for lunch on Saturday? I've got someone to have Joel so I'm going to really go for it. If you come it'll remind me to stop and eat. About twelve?'

'Smashing!' said Clo, brightening up.

'All right with you, Beth?'

Beth seemed surprised to be consulted. 'Yes. Please.'

'Good-oh. We'll catch up on everything then,' Ginny said, strapping Joel into his car seat. 'Oh, wait, I nearly forgot... Ow!'—she banged her head on the car door—'I've got a postcard for you, Clo, silly Lizzie couldn't remember your address so she sent it to us.'

She rubbed her head with one hand and fished about in her enormous hold-all with the other, eventually unearthing a seaside postcard.

'Oh great, thanks!'

Clo took it eagerly and put it in her pocket for later.

'Bye!' she shouted, but the car was already disappearing noisily through the gate.

They arrived home at the same time as Mam, who immediately began clucking over Beth's cast-off blanket. While she helped Beth upstairs Clo sat down on the doorstep to read her card. The picture on the front, of Brinkley beach in blazing sunshine, contrasted sharply with the message.

'Dear Clo,' it said, 'this is what it should look like here. We had the most amazing storm on Sunday night and we're still drying out! We're all in the same boat though (ha ha) and it's great to be here. Write to me soon, love Lizzie xxxx.'

Clo laughed. Picking up Mam's shopping bag, she went indoors, treating a surprised Mrs Kawalski to a dazzling smile on the way.

10

'What are you going to do with yourselves today?' Mam enquired at breakfast. 'It's going to be a scorcher by the looks of it.'

'Oh, I don't know—go to the park, I expect,' Clo said.

'That's nice, lovey, get all the fresh air you can—but make sure Beth's wrapped up!'

Beth raised her eyebrows slightly and Clo chuckled.

Mam rounded on her immediately. 'I'm serious, Chloe Olerenshaw! She's that frail a breeze would blow her over, we've got to take care of her. Now, here's some sandwiches and a pound—get something to go with them.'

'Mam, Mrs Lewis's asked us to have lunch with her on Saturday at the Wreck,' Clo said.

'The Wreck, what's that, a café?'

'No! It's what they call the Manse because it's such a mess. She's there nearly every day, decorating.'

'Gracious, is it really that bad? I suppose it was empty for a long time... but you didn't ought to let people hear you calling it a wreck, Clo, it's disrespectful.'

'All right, I won't. D'you think I could have a bit extra today? I want to write to Lizzie at Camp.'

Mam dug deep into her old purse. 'I'm a bit short till I get paid, but I think I can find you a fifty.'

'Thanks, Mam.'

While they waited for Albert, Clo took stock and decided that she needed to visit the library. Rushworth Library was one of her favourite places, a vast old-fashioned building with polished wooden tables and shelves and ancient, gurgling radiators. She loved it. She found two books to be returned and her spare tickets.

She made first for the Post Office, which was busier than usual because it was Pension Day. She heaved Beth's wheelchair up the step and through the door and joined a queue.

'Isn't it funny,' she reflected, 'whichever queue you choose, it's bound to be the one that moves slowest?'

Sure enough, they got stuck behind two people renewing

car tax, a process which seemed to take forever. As the man in front of them turned to go Clo pushed forward, accidentally catching his ankle with a wheel. A torrent of abuse was unleashed on her as the man hopped up and down clutching his bruised ankle.

'You're a menace with that thing!' he shouted. 'Shouldn't be allowed!'

Clo wanted to crawl away into a hole. Beth had done her usual trick of shutting her eyes and pretending to be asleep.

Some of the other customers took Clo's side:

'Shocking language to use to a little girl!'

'Some people don't half exaggerate!'

'If he had to cope with it he'd think different.'

She was grateful for their support, but by the time she raised her eyes to the counter again several people had taken advantage of the commotion and slipped in front.

'Blooming queue-jumpers!' she thought, crossly.

Eventually she got served with a picture postcard of Rushworth Town Hall and a first-class stamp. She had intended to write it there and then but decided it might be better to move on. The day had not started well but it was about to get worse.

They reached the library without too much trouble, though roadworks made progress difficult; the wheels easily stuck in the loose sand and today there was no friendly navvy to help them through. As they reached Library Square at last Clo stared in disbelief. Oh no! She'd forgotten that there was a long flight of steps leading up to revolving doors. She sat down on the bottom step and dropped her chin in her hands, almost in tears. It was only her books that kept her going these days. Escaping for an hour to Avonlea or Narnia was very important to her, but now she couldn't even do that.

She must have looked quite desolate because an old gentleman stopped and said, 'Cheer up lassie, it's never that bad!'

She recognized him as one of her supporters from the Post Office.

'It's impossible!' she burst out. 'I can't get the wheelchair up all these steps, can I? And I wanted to change my books, it's not fair!'

The old fellow looked round then moved closer. 'Don't you worry lassie, Ernie Earnshaw's here and he knows a way in!'

'Really, where? Tell me!' Clo was on her feet.

'You're not really supposed to use it,' he told her, 'it's a fire exit round the side. But they have it open on hot days and I sometimes slips in there when me rheumatics is too bad to get up all them steps.'

'Brilliant!' Clo cried.

Motioning to her to be quiet, Ernie led them round the side of the building.

'I'll go first,' he said, 'and tell you when her on the desk isn't watching. She's got a tongue like a razor blade, that one, a real dragon!'

Furtively he poked his head inside before sidling in through the fire door. A few seconds later Ernie's bony finger beckoned them into the dim interior. It was a bit of a tight squeeze with the chair but Clo got through. She parked Beth, got out her books, and skipped happily up the few steps to reception.

At that moment 'her on the desk' happened to glance down and spotted the wheelchair.

'Where did that invalid chair come from?' she demanded. 'Did you bring it inside?'

'Yes, Miss,' Clo admitted, trying to avoid the Dragon's piercing gaze.

'How did you get it in here, may I ask? It is entirely against the rules!'

'Through the side-door, Miss, I couldn't get it up the steps,' Clo explained, reasonably.

'The public is not allowed to use that door, it is an emergency exit!' the Dragon roared. 'I am continually reminding the staff not to leave it open.'

'But how else can people come in who can't use the steps?'

'They just can't!' snapped the Dragon. 'This is an old building, it isn't equipped for the handicapped.'

'Then perhaps it ought to be?' Clo ventured.

'Well I can't do anything about it,' the Dragon retorted, 'write to the Council if you've got a complaint but remove that wheelchair *now*!'

'I will write,' Clo lashed back, trembling, 'and I'll tell them how nasty you are to everybody too!'

Low mutterings of, 'That'd teach her,' 'Shame!' and, 'Old bag, wait till she's in a wheelchair!' drifted across from a group of elderly people reading the newspapers.

The Dragon glared and the mutterings ceased immediately.

Clo turned and fled without even giving her books in. She grabbed Beth and made for the exit.

Her accomplice whispered, 'Sorry, little girl, I didn't want to get you in a scrape...'

Clo shoved past the old man into the glaring sunlight, tears stinging her eyes. She rounded on her sister.

'You're always getting me into trouble!' she accused. 'It's all right for you sitting there with your eyes shut every time we have problems, everybody pities you, but I get the blame! It's not fair!'

Beth flinched under the attack. 'Clo, I...'

But Clo didn't want to discuss it; she shoved the chair violently towards the road, almost colliding with another wheelchair containing an old lady with pink hair—Mrs Wilkins, her friend from Savemore's.

'Hello my duckie!' she greeted Clo, oblivious of her distress. 'Hang on a minute, Iris,' she commanded her daughter, 'I know this young lady.'

'Hello, Mrs Wilkins,' Clo said, flatly, 'are you all right?'

'Very well, thanks dearie, and all the better for a spot of lovely weather. Have you finished school now?'

'Yes, we broke up on Friday.'

'Lovely, dearie. So many nice things to do at your age.'

She peered through her thick glasses at Beth. 'And I see you're helping them out at Whitegates, taking this little girl for a walk. You're a good girl!'

Clo looked squarely at Mrs Wilkins and at Iris. Whitegates was a residential school for disabled children not far away.

'Yes,' she said, 'that's right, I'm helping them out at Whitegates.'

'Lovely! Bye-bye then!'

Mrs Wilkins and Iris moved off, leaving Clo breathless with the knowledge of her betrayal. She had denied that Beth was her sister; she had let the two women believe that she was being kind and taking some inmate from the local home out for a walk, rather than seething with bitterness and resentment at being saddled with this, this... albatross, who prevented her from leading a normal life and denied her the freedom to do the things she wanted, no, *needed*, to do.

Beth was looking at her, a mixture of anger, pain and accusation in her eyes.

Clo gulped and looked away, knowing that she could never, ever look her in the eye again. She also knew that she couldn't

71

hang around here any more; Mrs Wilkins or Iris would be sure to mention their meeting to someone who would tell them the truth, then everyone would know what a hateful person she was.

There was a large map on a board near the library. Clo got her bearings and chose a back way to Brickfields, feeling more desolate and more of an outcast than ever. There was no market on Thursday, the space was empty. They went further, stopping at a newsagent's for some drinks. Clo spotted a park in the distance—a thicket of tall trees, geraniums and green railings—and she made for that. On the gate it said, 'Brickfields Memorial Gardens. Dogs Must Be On Leads.' Just inside the gate was a war memorial with a lady waving a wreath on top, and lists of names engraved on the sides. Past the monument could be seen the glint of water—a large artificial lake with well-grown rhododendron bushes and wooden shelters to sit in round it; it seemed deserted. This was ideal, Clo thought, just the place to hide. She selected the shelter furthest from the road, parked Beth outside in the sun and silently handed her her lunch. Then she withdrew into the shadows at the back of the shelter and fished the postcard from her pocket.

She wrote: 'Dear Lizzie, Greetings from sunny Rushworth! Sorry you got wet, we had an amazing thunderstorm too! Being stuck with You-know-who all day is beastly and everybody is horrid but we are having lunch with your Mum on Saturday which will be great. Come back soon, love Clo xxx. PS our address is...'

She put the card aside, opened her sandwiches and stared out across the lake, pretending she was alone. She remembered that tomorrow was Friday and Beth had her appointment at the hospital—wonderful, a day to herself! She began to relax.

'Aagh!'

She was startled by something cold and wet touching her hand. Looking down she met the liquid brown eyes of a hairy little dog gazing up at her appealingly. She let out her breath and laughed.

'Hello, dog, I thought you were a slug or something! Are you hungry?'

She broke off a corner of her sandwich and the dog wolfed it down as if it hadn't eaten for a week. They shared the rest of the sandwich and the next and, finally, a bar of chocolate.

The little dog nuzzled her hand, hoping for more.

'Sorry boy, that's the lot,' she said. 'You're not supposed to be in here without a lead, are you lost?'

Her fingers found a collar buried under the fur, with a name tag attached.

'Daffy Aquarius Pots, Brickfields,' she read.

Odd sort of a name. Obviously he belonged to somebody called Pots nearby.

'So you're not a stray at all,' she accused, wagging her finger, 'you've just been having me on for a free feed!'

The dog woofed joyfully.

'I don't mind,' Clo said. 'Alright, Daffy Pots, do you want to play?'

She found a stick to throw for the dog, who was beside himself with pleasure. Even Beth chuckled at his antics. Clo kept throwing the stick and the dog tirelessly brought it back to her. Finally she accidentally threw it in the direction of the water and watched helplessly as Daffy flung himself into the lake to retrieve it. He was back in a moment, soaked through. As she bent to pick up the stick he shook himself, showering her with water.

'Ooh, you little terror,' she laughed, 'stop it!'

She brushed herself down and prepared to go home, her mood lighter. She had to run back to the shelter for the postcard and returned to find Daffy nuzzling up to Beth who was happily stroking his head. He accompanied them to the park gates where he rubbed against Clo's knee one last time and, without a backward glance, trotted off in the opposite direction.

Clo pushed Beth back to Raglan Street, posting Lizzie's card on the way. She limped in her tight trainers—she'd done a lot of walking in the past few days—and wondered if it would be tactful to ask Mam for a new pair.

Clo sat on the doorstep watching for the ambulance. She was avoiding Beth. Still ashamed of yesterday, she was afraid to speak to her—no, afraid that Beth might speak to *her* and voice her feelings of rejection and anger at her sister's denial. She shivered in spite of the warm sun. She must pull herself together, she only had a few hours' freedom and she meant to put them to good use—the library for one thing. But it was no longer a simple thing to pop into the library and change her books, was it? What if the Dragon was on duty again? What if she decided to confiscate her tickets for being rude? But she had to return her books some time so there seemed no alternative but to face the music.

'But what if,' Clo thought, 'she didn't recognize me?'

A plan began to formulate in her mind: if she was in disguise, then there was less chance of detection—the Dragon hadn't checked in her books and didn't know her name. Of course, this meant she would probably have to go in disguise ever after, but she'd face that problem when she had to. Delighted with her strategy, Clo was still hugging her knees and grinning to herself when a vehicle drew up and a solid pair of black boots planted themselves in front of her.

'Good morning, young lady! You look pleased with yourself—won the Lottery?'

She looked up at the ambulance driver.

'No! Sorry, I was miles away. She's ready, just go up.'

The driver beckoned to his mate and they went upstairs, emerging a couple of minutes later with Beth between them.

'We'll bring her back around half-past two, m'dear, you'll be in, won't you?'

'Yes, of course,' Clo answered, looking at the pavement, 'thanks, bye.'

She dashed upstairs. Wrenching open the wardrobe door she excavated the heap of fabrics, jumble finds and play clothes inside, emerging at intervals to inspect a likely garment and throw it back onto the pile. She considered an old dancing dress of Mam's, green net with sequins, but decided it might attract more attention than she wanted. No, it had to be something more normal. What had she been wearing yesterday? Shorts, T-shirt and trainers, right. She chose her red dungarees, her Rasta hat and her red duffel coat, a pair of wellington boots and sunglasses. She tucked all her hair under the hat and squinted at herself in the mirror: she looked like an oversized Paddington Bear. Excellent! She put her spectacles in her pocket, gathered up her books and left the house, convinced nobody would ever recognize her.

Before she was half way down the High Street Clo had begun to cook in the heavy coat. She felt the sweat form on her scalp beneath the woolly hat and her feet burned in the rubber boots. Still, it was worth it. She plodded on. At the library, her courage momentarily seeped away into her boiling boots. Might not the Dragon's steely glare penetrate even the most cunning disguise? She tried to peek sideways through the revolving doors but the sun on the glass made it difficult to see inside. She sat down on the top step, feeling very hot and bothered.

Suddenly, a hand grasped her shoulder! She jumped up, scattering books, her heart in her mouth.

'Clo! Why ever are you dressed like that on a baking hot day? You'll melt!'

She squinted fearfully through her sunglasses; Howard Lewis grinned down at her—so much for the disguise.

'Hello, Mr Lewis, I was, er, just going to change my books,' she said.

'I can see that,' he said, picking them up, 'but why the disguise? You *are* in disguise, aren't you?'

Clo removed her sunglasses and wiped the sweat from her forehead.

'C'mon, Clo! We're both artistes—you can tell me.'

He sat down and patted the step beside him. His willingness to sit in the dust and talk, in his dog-collar and everything, gave Clo the confidence to explain.

'I had a bit of an argument with the Dragon yesterday— she's the one in charge and she's terribly fierce. All the old men are scared of her.'

'I know the one!' Howard laughed. 'If you even cough she looks like she'd throw you to the lions! I see. So you and she had a little altercation and now you're trying to sneak in in disguise, is that it?'

'Yes, only it's obviously not going to work because you knew it was me straight away.'

'Ah, don't be so sure,' Howard said, 'remember I'm a trained actor and I notice funny little things about people—trick of the trade. I admit I did recognize the jazzy hat but I *would* have been fooled except for one thing: when you're worried, Clo, you screw your mouth up in a particular way—like this.'

He imitated Clo's 'worried' look which made her laugh.

'And that, my dear Watson, was a dead give-away!'

Clo made a mental note to do something about the awful expression, but she was encouraged to hear that her disguise wasn't a complete failure.

Howard stood up. 'Well, I've got to collect a book. If you'd like a bodyguard you can come in with me. If it seems like you're about to be rumbled, just hand me your books and run and I'll get your tickets for you, OK?'

'OK, boss!' Clo replaced the sunglasses.

They strode nonchalantly in and up to the desk. One of the nice young assistants was in charge and she only looked slightly quizzically at Clo.

Howard couldn't resist asking, 'Is the Drag... Chief Librarian not here today?'

'No Sir, it's her day off, did you want to speak to her particularly?'

'No, no, it's nothing important. I'll catch her some other time,' he said, looking meaningfully at Clo, who giggled.

'Right, you go and get your books,' he said, 'then maybe I can interest you in a milk shake at Gino's?'

She nodded enthusiastically.

'They have air-conditioning there, you'll be more comfortable!'

Fifteen minutes later Clo had got rid of hat, coat and dark glasses and was sitting in Gino's with a pineapple milk shake; she couldn't do much about the boots but she felt cooler already. Howard spooned the froth off a cappuchino. 'Want to tell me what your argument with the Dragon was about?'

Clo wasn't sure. How much could she tell without confessing all? She thought she could probably trust Howard. Weren't ministers supposed to keep people's awful secrets to themselves, like doctors?

'Well,' she began, 'the thing is, it's impossible to get a wheelchair up the library steps and Ernie Earnshaw—he's an old man I met—told me about the fire exit...'

She recounted the whole escapade to Howard, finishing

with their rapid exit from the building.

'Mmm,' he said, thoughtfully, 'it's a problem, this lack of access to public buildings—the Town Hall is nearly as bad, and most of the cinemas in Rushworth too. It's outrageous that disabled people can't enjoy the same amenities as the rest of us, pure discrimination.'

'Yes, well, the Dragon said there was nothing she could do and we'd have to complain to the Council. Then she threw us out.'

'Poor old Clo! I'll bet you felt pretty angry and frustrated, didn't you?'

Clo confessed, 'Yes, I was so mad because it was the second time that morning I'd had problems and I'm afraid... I'm afraid I took it out on Beth—I yelled at her that it was all her fault I couldn't even change my library books. Well, she just closes her eyes and pretends to be asleep all the time and I know she's not!'

She expected Howard to be shocked but he just said, 'Rather unkind when Beth can't help the way she is, but I can understand your feelings in the circumstances.'

She could have left it there but something made Clo want to get it all off her chest. She studied the yellow scum in the bottom of her glass.

'But there was more—worse than that.'

'Oh, what?'

'I pretended she wasn't my sister,' Clo gulped out, feeling her throat go tight at the memory. 'We saw Mrs Wilkins and she's got bad eyes. She thought I was looking after one of the handicapped kids from Whitegates and I said yes, because I didn't want her to think Beth was anything to do with me and... and she said I was a good girl!'

She was struggling to stop herself crying.

Howard whipped out a giant handkerchief carried for just such emergencies and said, 'Here, get it all out!'

When Clo's sobs subsided Howard stood up.

'I think we both need a drink,' he said in an American gangster voice, 'same again, lady?' And without waiting for a reply he strode to the counter for refills.

Clo sucked on another milk shake—with ice-cream this time—and mopped her eyes with the sodden hankie. Howard sat back with a black coffee and wished he still smoked.

'Poor old Clo,' he said.

Then, 'So what are you going to do now?'

'Do? You mean I ought to go and tell Mrs Wilkins and Iris that I lied?'

'Well, they're bound to realize sooner or later, but no, I mean what will you do about Beth?'

'I don't know. I'm stuck with her but I can't bear to look at her now. I know I was horrid but, well, I can't explain to her, she doesn't understand.'

'Doesn't she? Just because she doesn't say much doesn't mean she doesn't feel things deeply, you know.'

Clo had sort of known that; and she remembered the hurt expression on Beth's face.

'Do you think you could possibly say sorry?'

She thought for a minute. 'No,' she replied, frankly, 'I don't think I can. Is that awful?'

'No, it's just the way things stand at the moment, something for you to work on,' Howard said. 'But next time you need to yell at somebody—yell at God.'

'At God?' Clo stared at him.

'Yes. He can take it and he won't mind, I promise. Well, I must get on, Ginny's looking forward to seeing you both tomorrow. You know, we really ought to tackle somebody about disabled access—you'd be an ideal person to do something, Clo, you've got first-hand experience of some of the problems now.'

He left the suggestion hanging in the simmering air outside Gino's Café.

Clo bundled up all her unnecessary clothing and went home. The situation hadn't been resolved but she felt better for having shared it with somebody. She looked at her watch. Twelve-thirty. Great. Two hours' solid reading before she was back on duty again.

She was spared any forced intimacy with her sister that afternoon because the ambulance was late and Mam already home. After tea Jenny and Janice turned up to see Beth just as Mam and Eric were going out to view a flat.

Janice said, 'Hello, Chloe, Mummy said you'd been into the Oxfam Shop on Tuesday.'

Clo didn't feel like discussing it. She just said, 'Yes. Well, I'll leave you with her, then,' and escaped to the bedroom where she spent an hour making a Welcome card for the Lewises' new home, sticking scraps of sari material onto a drawing of a rainbow with 'Wreck, Sweet Wreck' written under it. Better not let Mam see that! She was still engrossed in her artwork when her grandmother opened the door.

'There you are,' she said, 'now why can't you do your cutting out on the kitchen table? Come and say goodbye to Jenny and Janice.'

Clo hid the card and went through.

'Have you had a nice time, girls?' Mam was asking.

'Yes, thank you, Mrs Appleby,' Jenny answered, nicely, 'we looked at my sister's wedding photos and watched "Coronation Street",' as if to assure her that they hadn't touched on any forbidden subjects.

'Well, she certainly looks better for seeing you,' Mam remarked, 'come again soon—we'll let you know our new address when we move.'

'Are we going to have that flat?' asked Clo.

'No, not that one,' Eric said, 'it was in a right state and the stairs were worse than here. Never mind, summat'll turn up.'

Next morning Clo was out of bed putting the finishing touches to her card before anyone else was awake. Even though her friends hadn't officially moved in, she decided she would give it to them today to cheer them on. She wrapped it carefully in a sheet of drawing paper and sealed it with silver tape left over from Christmas.

Mam puffed upstairs before going to work, waving a fruit cake.

'I just popped round to Patel's for this, lovey, take it with you to the Manse for your lunch.'

'But Mam...'

'No buts, it's just a little contribution. Now, behave yourself.'

'Yes, Mam!'

'And don't outstay your welcome, I expect Mrs Lewis is very busy. It's very good of her to find time for you.'

'Yes, Mam!'

'And mind you wrap up, the weather's changed again—looks like rain.'

Clo was impatient to be off. Beth sat at the table, reading a magazine; she looked quite normal. For a minute Clo could imagine it was the real Beth sitting there and that nothing had ever happened to change her. She looked away and concentrated on squeezing her feet into her trainers—bother! She'd meant to mention them to Mam.

At last it was time to go and Eric, who was going through the To Let ads in the paper with a red biro, looked up.

'D'you mind if I walk as far as the Manse with you?' he said, 'I'm going to do the rounds of the newsagents, see if there's any flats advertised in the windows.'

Clo didn't want to share Ginny with other people but she felt sorry for Eric, having to spend Saturday flat-hunting, so she said, 'No of course not, you can have a look at the Wreck.'

'Don't let Mabel hear you say that!' Eric chuckled, 'she thinks the minister's house is holy ground, like Chapel!'

12

Ginny spotted them from an upstairs window and waved her paintbrush at them.

'It's open!' she yelled.

The hallway was strewn with old sheets and pieces of plastic.

'Sorry about all this,' she said, 'a vain attempt to confine the paint to the walls. I've finished the Golden Room, come and see, it's wonderful.'

She led them into the lounge. On a gloomy day like today it positively glowed.

'Even in the bleak midwinter we shall have sunshine!' Ginny said.

Even Eric, who was a magnolia-and-white man when it came to decorating, had to admit it was very cheerful.

'Do have a look round, Mr Appleby,' Ginny said. 'Can you stay for lunch?'

'No, thank you, Missus, I mustn't stop. Eh, look at that garden, I'd dearly love a piece that size!'

'Yes, it will be lovely when it's tamed, though I confess I rather like it wild!' said Ginny. 'In fact, would you like to rescue some of those gorgeous yellow roses for Mrs Appleby? They're wasted with nobody here.'

'Very kind of you,' Eric said, 'Mabel's soft on flowers.'

'Take Beth with you,' Ginny suggested, 'you haven't seen our jungle yet, have you, Beth? There's a sweet little stone bench near the bottom.'

Clever Ginny! Clo realized that this had been for her benefit.

'Come and see what I'm doing upstairs,' Ginny said.

They dodged under planks and ladders and went upstairs to the newly-painted attic.

Ginny said, 'I hear you've been having a few adventures. People aren't very helpful, are they, on the whole? I used to get so mad trying to heave a pushchair on and off buses with a screaming infant and a week's shopping!'

'Joel?'

'No, I was thinking of Mary actually. Pushchairs weren't so streamlined in those days, and we didn't have a car.'

Clo giggled as she pictured Mary as a screaming infant.

'Don't tell her I told you! Seriously though, Howard tells me it's getting to you—don't worry, he didn't go into details, that wouldn't be professional, but he did tip me the wink.'

Clo sighed. 'Yes, it's true, I've been horrid to Beth. It's so difficult—I can't think of her as... Beth, I mean, *my sister* Beth, any more. It's not just the problems with the chair, it's like pushing a stranger round all day!'

Ginny pushed back her hair, leaving a streak of paint across her forehead.

'I see. How did you feel towards her before the accident?'

That was easy! 'Oh, she was so clever, always winning medals and things, and she was pretty and lots of fun.'

'But how did you *feel* about her?'

'I thought she was great! I was a bit jealous sometimes because I'm hopeless at sports but I was proud of her—I loved her.'

Ginny brought her paint-smudged face closer to Clo's. Her eyes had gold specks in them, like a lioness, Clo thought.

'Exactly: you admired her, you were proud of her, you loved her. Clo—that person in the wheelchair may have changed on the surface but inside she's still the Beth you loved and admired. She isn't some monster from outer space, she's the same person only she can't do the things she used to do. Do you understand?'

Clo hadn't really thought of it like that. She nodded.

'Clo, I hope and pray that one day Beth will be able to do all those things again, but she needs help and time to get there.'

'And in the meantime, I'm stuck with her,' said Clo, gloomily.

'And in the meantime, she's stuck with you! Remember that, she can't get away from you either. One way and another, kid, you're in this thing together, so you'd best make it as easy for yourselves as possible.'

Clo sighed. 'Mr Lewis asked me if I could say sorry to her for... for being awful the other day, but I can't, not yet.'

'You could always say sorry to God,' Ginny suggested.

'Would that do as well?'

'It's a good start.'

'I'll think about it.' Clo studied the paint-spattered floor.

'But no breast-beating!' Ginny cried, 'you're no good to anybody feeling guilty and sorry for yourself—life's too short! We all fail; if we didn't, how on earth would we ever learn anything? I think you've reached the lowest ebb and things can only get better. I'm starving, let's go and find some grub.'

Lunch was a picnic on the lounge floor, eaten with fingers because Ginny had forgotten the cutlery. They ate French bread with seeds on it and smelly cheese and big chunks of fruit cake, washed down with lemonade out of the bottle— Mam wouldn't have approved. Ginny was delighted with Clo's card and put it on the mantelpiece.

'Wherever did you find these gorgeous bits of material?' she asked, stroking the purple silk in the rainbow.

'My friend Mr Rashid at the Sari Shop gave them to me years ago. I save them for special things.'

'I'm honoured,' said Ginny. 'You must introduce me to Mr Rashid some time. I couldn't half fancy a dress this colour— or even a sari!'

Clo was just relaxing into this pleasant atmosphere when the alarm on Ginny's watch went off.

'Goodness, is it that time already?' she cried, leaping up. 'I've got to collect Joel. Sorry girls, got to shut up shop.'

Clo was disappointed. She'd hoped to stay all day.

'Where will you go this afternoon?' Ginny asked, gathering her things together.

'Brickfields Park, probably,' Clo said, 'I found it the other day, it's got a lake and things.'

'Brickfields—couldn't be better! Do me a favour? I need to get a message to the pottery over there. I'm having a plate made for my friend Molly's baby with his name and date of birth and so on and they're firing this weekend—would you mind taking them the details?'

'No, of course not.'

Ginny gave her an envelope with an address on it.

'Bless you. Kim isn't on the phone and you'll save me a trip... you can't miss it, it's the Old Bakery on the corner of Victoria and Albert.'

She noted Clo's downcast expression.

'Clo, cheer up love, I'm sorry to hustle you off like this. Life will be much easier after we've moved—forgive me?' she begged.

''Course!'

Ginny hugged her and was screeching out of the gates five seconds later.

Clo looked at her watch.

Nearly one o'clock. Another two hours to fill before there'd be anyone at home.

She sighed. Everybody had promised to help and support her but they were all so busy doing other things: Mam, Eric, Ginny, the girls. Even Miss Redmond. Clo felt deserted.

In Brickfields she stopped outside Eccles' newspaper shop to look at the advertisements in the window.

FOR SALE, she read, BEAUTIFUL IVORY WEDDING DRESS SIZE 16, NEVER WORN.

'I wonder why?' she thought.

AQUARIUS POTS HAND-THROWN EARTHENWARE, read another.

Where had she seen that name before?

LOVELY KITTENS FREE TO GOOD HOME...

No, no flats to rent. She narrowed her eyes so that the postcards and the multi-coloured jars of sweets fuzzed out, leaving only their own reflections in the window. Clo's wore that worried expression Howard had told her about. It was difficult to tell what Beth saw. Afraid their eyes might meet Clo shoved open the shop door and went inside. Mr Eccles' bald head popped up from behind the counter. She rummaged in her pocket for her money.

'A packet of pastilles, please, and one of those liquorice lollies in the window. No, no need to put them in a bag.'

Mr Eccles clanged the old-fashioned cash register.

'Not so warm out today, is it?' he remarked, recognizing Clo from earlier in the week.

But Clo wasn't in the mood for conversation. 'No, it's not,' she answered shortly.

She tugged open the door and was gone before Mr Eccles could detain her further.

'Now there's an unhappy little girl,' he said to himself.

He craned his neck and watched through the window as Clo crammed the lolly into her mouth and handed the sweets to the girl in the wheelchair.

'Oh, innit sad?' a voice beside them said.

'A real shame,' another voice agreed.

Two women about to enter the shop had stopped and were regarding Beth with pity.

'Such a pretty little thing as well, how dreadful for the parents!' said the first.

'It's usually in the genes, poor little lass,' replied her friend, knowingly.

They spoke sympathetically but loudly, as though neither Beth nor Clo could hear them. Clo scowled and jolted the chair past them, narrowly missing their feet.

'How dare they,' she thought, 'talking as if we're both deaf—or daft!'

Suddenly she couldn't cope with all this, not today. She broke into a run across the road and into the park, swerved round the war memorial like a racing driver and along the edge of the lake to the end shelter. She peered inside.

'Good, it's empty,' she breathed.

Leaving Beth outside she retreated into the shadows and threw herself down on the bench, panting. She felt safe here from staring eyes. The view today was depressing, grey clouds hid the sun. The breeze that ruffled the surface of the lake was cool but the air inside the shelter was warm and stale. Clo was tired, her feet hurt and she felt the weight of her responsibilities more than ever. She dozed in the stuffy shelter and dreamt of the little dog that came last time and licked her hand. She could feel its rough little tongue on her skin. She opened her eyes and as she did so, the sun broke through the clouds like a burning spotlight. It seemed to reach in and find her right there at the back of the shelter; it struck her full in the face so that she threw up her hand against the glare; she felt as though she had been pointed out, discovered.

'Here she is,' it seemed to say, 'hiding away among the shadows, wallowing in self-pity again!'

Clo shrank back against the rough wood of the shelter, feeling like an accused person confronted with her misdeeds. The moment of alarm passed. The light still shone but it no longer felt threatening, more like an invitation to bring things out into the open.

She heard herself speaking softly and urgently under her breath to—well, she wasn't sure who to, but Someone out there, maybe God, who seemed like they might be in control of everything.

'I'm sorry,' she said, 'I'm not doing very well, am I? It's just that I've felt so pushed out and taken over by Beth and I know that's rotten because she can't help it. In a way it's been easier to think of her like the albatross in that poem, a drag, a dead-weight. But Ginny's right—she's exactly the same person as before, not an enemy alien. And she needs me. It's very difficult, but please, help me to love her and help her. I don't feel like it or really want to do it, but I will try, honestly.'

A sort of quiet calm seemed to fill the shelter. The light had diminished to a warm glow and Clo felt a great sense of relief, a weight off her mind—as though she had been heard and it was all right. Ginny had said things must get better...

'Oh, goodness, Ginny!' she said aloud.

She leapt to her feet—she was supposed to be delivering that message to the pottery! She felt in her pocket for the envelope. Holding it to the light she read: Kim Bell, Aquarius Pots, The Old Bakery, Victoria Road, Brickfields. Aquarius Pots again! Why, it was the name of the pottery, not the dog! She looked at her watch—nearly two. They'd better get a move on, she still had to find out where the Old Bakery was.

Mr Eccles was just about to close. He looked up with interest as Clo entered his shop for the second time that afternoon.

'Aquarius Pots? Easy, carry on up the hill, first left along Victoria Road and it's on a sharp corner with Albert Avenue, you can't miss it, lots of pretty coloured things in the window.'

Clo thanked him.

Mr Eccles was right, she couldn't have missed that shop in a million years. It was, as he had said, on a very sharp corner, a thin, triangular building with windows on both sides with the original enamelled Hovis signs along the top. Clo gazed at little stained-glass plaques hanging in the windows, glittering crystals on invisible threads, revolving, sending out rainbow-coloured sparks, and stickers with intricate Celtic designs. On the shelves were pots of all shapes, everyday kitchenware and mugs, ornate bowls and garden planters, and ornaments like little jewels, cushioned in sawdust and dried flowers. She was fascinated.

She could have stood for hours enjoying the display but she hadn't forgotten her errand. She pushed Beth round to the double doors at the point of the building. There was a small ramp instead of steps—that made a change! She opened one of the doors and an old-fashioned brass bell jingled above her head. As she backed the wheelchair in somebody held open the other door for her. She looked up into a dark face crowned with brown sausages.

The owner of the wonderful hairstyle grinned hugely, bowed and said, 'Allow me, Madame!' in a very refined voice.

Then, in a quite different voice, 'Dig that hat, gal, you got another one like that for me?'

'Oh, sorry!' Clo said, 'I only found one, at a jumble sale, but

86

I could look out for another if you like.'

'Hey, I'm kidding you!' he said, 'I'm just off out but can I help?'

'Is Kim in?' she asked. 'Only I've got a message.'

'Sure is, through the back—keep happy!'

Clo paused, taking in the interior of the shop. So many interesting things to look at, and a smell that reminded her of Mr Rashid's. Beth liked it too. Both of them were attracted to a little round pot with a turquoise-blue glaze displayed alone on a stand in the middle of the floor. For a brief moment their eyes met in mutual appreciation. Clo hurriedly got out the envelope and moved towards a bead curtain, through which came a soft whirring sound. She pushed it aside to reveal the back of a slight figure with a long blonde pony-tail, in jeans and an old denim shirt, sitting on a high stool at a wheel where a lump of clay was being transformed into something quite different.

Clo cleared her throat. 'Er, excuse me, Miss.'

'Shan't be a minute.'

The voice which answered her was deeper than she expected. The wheel stopped and the figure turned. She gasped: a man with a blond beard, piercing blue eyes and a gold earring in one ear, sat grinning at her.

Clo was confused. 'Oh! I'm sorry, I thought...'

'What for? An understandable mistake, and not for the first time!'

'Are you Kim Bell?'

'Indeed I am, what can I do for you?'

'I've brought you a message from Mrs Lewis, the name of her friend's baby.'

'Ah yes, Ginny's plate and only just in time because we're firing tonight.'

Kim took the envelope from Clo and went over to a bench piled high with plates and pots which looked as though they had been painted with emulsion paint. Clo noticed that he limped.

'Know anything about pottery, Clo?'

Clo shook her head.

'Interested?'

'Oh yes, I like making things.' She wondered how he knew her name.

'Right, I'll show you how we do this...' He stopped and listened. 'Somebody with you?'

'Only Beth. My sister.'

'Only?' Kim looked searchingly at Clo.

He stuck his head through the curtain. 'Hi there, Beth, you OK for a minute? Be with you in a mo, only this door's a bit narrow for your chair.'

He turned back to Clo. 'All these things you see have been fired—baked—in the kiln once already, they're what is known as biscuit-fired...'

He explained that they had been dipped in a glaze solution which would turn bright and shiny after they had been fired again. He picked up a plate and a brush and expertly wrote 'James Alan Marshall' and the date around the edge, finishing it with a flourish.

'Ooh, that's clever!' Clo said, 'I wish I could do that. What colour will it come out?'

'This will be cream and brown, traditional earthenware colours,' Kim said. 'Come back next week and see the finished article.'

'Yes, please.'

'Now, let me introduce myself to Beth.'

In the shop Kim pulled up a low stool and sat beside Beth's chair so that he could speak to her face-to-face.

'Ginny and I were at Art College together,' he told them, 'she said she might send a couple of young friends along one of these days.'

Oh, so Ginny had told him about them. 'How much?' Clo wondered to herself.

Beth was still looking at the turquoise pot.

'Like it?' Kim asked.

'It's lovely!' both girls answered at once.

'I am rather pleased with that glaze, I must say,' he said.

He picked up the pot and turned it in his hand.

'This is called raku pottery,' he explained, 'it's not fired like the others but in a special little wood fire out in the back yard—very risky—sometimes it doesn't work and you end up with lumps of blackened clay. But sometimes something comes out that you couldn't possibly have predicted, like this.'

He handed the pot to Beth who cupped it carefully in her hands, stroking its smooth surface. Clo felt slightly jealous that her sister should be entrusted with such a precious object. 'How much is it?' she asked.

She had some birthday money in the Post Office and thought she might be able to buy it.

'Who knows?' said Kim, mysteriously. 'It's worth everything and nothing. You can't put a price on something like that. Beauty is priceless, really. Fancy a cup of tea?'

They both nodded, grateful for an excuse to stay a little longer in this magical place. 'Lapsang Souchong, Gunpowder or Dahjeeling?' Kim asked. 'Or maybe something herbal? Mint, chamomile...'

Clo gasped, 'I don't know, we only ever have ordinary at home!'

Kim smiled. 'Then you have many pleasurable new experiences ahead of you! Tell you what, you can try a different one every time you come. You will come again, won't you?'

'Yes, please!' Clo said.

She chose chamomile tea because it sounded soothing.

'Beth can choose next time,' said Kim.

He went into the back room to put the kettle on while Clo wandered around the shop.

'You can pick things up,' he said, poking his head through the curtain.

Clo had been dying to, but Mam had always taught them not to touch things in shops. She held the little raku bowls, stroked some ornate Indian embroidery hanging from the stairs, and sniffed a rack of incense sticks; she set a set of wind-chimes tinkling and traced a never-ending snake which decorated a garden pot. For Beth the beautiful turquoise pot held her whole attention.

Kim came back with three hand-made mugs and a plate of flapjacks on a Chinese tray.

'Highly recommended,' he said, 'from the wholefood shop down the road.'

Suddenly there was a scratching at the shop door.

'That sounds like Daffy,' Kim laughed, 'must have smelt the flapjacks!'

He opened the door and the dog bounded in and leapt straight onto Clo's knee.

'I think you must have met before,' Kim said.

'Yes,' Clo gasped, fending off Daffy's licks, 'in the park. When I saw his collar I thought that was all his name—Daffy Aquarius Pots.'

'That sounds most distinguished,' Kim said, 'especially for a scruffy little so-and-so like Daffs!'

'He's lovely,' Clo said, 'he really cheered me up the other day.'

'Yes, he's good like that,' Kim said.

The bell jingled again and the sausage-haired youth came in.

'Hey man, soon as me back is turned you starts a-partyin'! See how I'm treated?' he appealed to the girls, who giggled. 'How'm I goin' to sweat over a hot kiln all night without me flapjacks?'

Kim laughed. 'I think you'll cope!' he said. 'This is Isaac, my trainee, and he's just been home for one of his mum's gigantic lunches!'

Isaac snapped his fingers, 'Ha! Discovered!'

'To work!' Kim said, getting up off the floor.

To the girls he said, 'Stay a bit longer if you like.'

'We'd better get home,' Clo said. 'Can we really come back?'

'Whenever you like. Come on Tuesday if you want to see the kiln unpacked.'

'I will,' said Clo.

'You too, Beth?' Kim asked.

'Yes, please, I'd love to,' Beth nodded happily.

She held out the blue pot and Kim replaced it carefully on its stand.

'Will you see Ginny?' he asked, opening the doors.

'Yes, at Chapel tomorrow,' said Clo.

'Tell her that, all being well, her plate will be ready on Tuesday.'

'I'll tell her,' Clo said, 'we'll see you then.'

A little way down the road she turned. Isaac, with Daffy in his arms, and Kim stood in the doorway, waving. Clo felt strange. She realized that she was feeling things that she hadn't felt for a long time—excited and happy, really deeply happy, as though there was something nice to look forward to.

13

Clo could hardly wait to go back to the pottery on Tuesday. Kim and Isaac were busy unpacking what looked like a huge oven at the back of the workshop.

'Hi there,' Kim called, 'you're just in time—come and look.'
Clo bounded forward.

'You too, Beth?' he asked.

'I can't really,' Beth said, 'not with...'

'Sorry, I really must get this doorway widened. Won't be long, have a look at this while you're waiting.'

He handed her a colourful crafts magazine from the counter.

In the workshop plates, bowls and mugs covered every surface. They looked very different from the dull, chalky objects Clo had seen waiting to be fired: shiny greens, yellows, browns and creams glowed everywhere. She gazed at the transformation.

'Magic, innit?' said Isaac.

'Yes,' she breathed, 'they're beautiful.'

'This is Ginny's plate,' Kim showed her, 'it's come out well. Is she going to call for it, do you know?'

'She said she'd try to come this afternoon, but if not, could I take it?'

'Sure,' Kim said. 'OK Isaac, time for a well-earned break, get that kettle on, man!'

While the water boiled Kim said quietly to Clo, 'Tell me about Beth, can she walk at all?'

'Yes, if somebody helps her.'

'Is it her back?'

'No, her head.'

'How do you mean?'

'We had a car crash and she banged her head. It's called a Reversible Brain Injury, it's supposed to get better eventually.'

'And that was how long ago?'

'Before Christmas, more than six months.'

'And she's been in that wheelchair ever since?'

'Yes.'

'Hey, that's rough. Do you take her out every day, Clo?'

'Yes, since the holidays started and Mam went back to work.'

'Can't she get about by herself at all?'

'No of course not, I told you, she can't walk on her own.'

'I realize that,' Kim said, 'but most wheelchair users can propel themselves with their hands—there are usually rims on the wheels. I'll have a look at Beth's chair later, see what it can do.'

He stuck his head into the shop. 'What kind of tea, Beth? Your turn to choose.'

No answer.

'Beth?'

Beth looked up from the pottery article in which she was engrossed. 'Mmm?'

Kim laughed. 'You were miles away! What kind of tea do you fancy?'

'Lapsang whatever-it-is, please, that sounded nice.'

Clo was surprised: Beth seldom strung more than two words together in her hearing, but here in the pottery it was as if she had found her tongue.

'Lapsang Souchong it is then,' he said. 'All right in here?'

'Yes thanks,' Beth said, 'this is really interesting.'

Clo collected the mugs while Kim made the tea.

'I expect you've discovered some of the problems of getting a wheelchair about the place?' he said.

'Yes, it's awful,' Clo burst out, 'steps everywhere, especially the library—that's hopeless—and most shops. At least you've got a little slope instead of steps. I wish other places were the same.'

'Well, you see, I understand some of the difficulties.'

He stuck out his left leg and Clo saw he wore a metal brace attached to his boot.

'I had polio when I was a kid, and I was in a wheelchair for years until somebody had the good sense to get me out of it. It was terribly frustrating for a young lad who wanted to climb trees and play football. So you see, I understand how it must feel for Beth. Has she talked to you about it?'

'Er, no,' Clo said, 'we don't talk much.'

'I see.'

Kim thought for a minute.

Then he said, 'Tell you what, Clo, why don't you grab a bit of time to yourself this afternoon and give me the opportunity to get to know Beth?'

Privately Clo thought Kim wouldn't get very far with her sister but she said, 'That would be great. Are you sure it's all right?'

'Sure,' Kim said, 'you deserve a break from each other.'

When they had drunk their tea, Kim said casually, 'Clo, will you do me a favour? Pop down to the butcher's at the end of the road and ask for a bag of bones for Daffy. Then on your way back you can call at the wholefood shop for some carrot cake for us all.'

He gave Clo a fiver.

'Take your time, no rush.'

Clo went gratefully. She collected Daffy's bones—he appeared to have a standing order—and called at Mr Eccles' for a postcard to send to Lizzie. She picked a photograph of Brickfields Park in 1930.

'Oh, it had a bandstand then?' she said, examining it.

'It did that. I can remember going to hear the brass bands when I was a young 'un,' Mr Eccles told her, 'those were the days.'

'Do you sell stamps?' Clo asked.

'Book of four?'

'I only need one, I haven't got enough money for four.'

'No problem,' Mr Eccles said, kindly, 'I think I've got an odd one somewhere. On your own today, are you?'

'Yes, Beth's at the pottery with Kim.'

'He's all right is Kim. A bit unusual, like, but all right.'

Clo leaned on a litter-bin outside to write her postcard.

'Dear Lizzie,' she wrote, 'things are looking up. I have met some amazing people called Kim and Izak. They have a shop called Aquarius Pots and a dog called Daffy. When you get back I will take you to see them. How is Camp? Love Clo xxx.'

She posted the card and wandered along the road, looking in shop windows, enjoying being on her own for a change. The wholefood shop was called Food for Thought and was almost as exciting as the pottery, with dozens of jars of dried beans and grains and herbs. The assistants all seemed to have rainbow-coloured hair and several earrings. The one who served Clo only looked about sixteen and had a little jewel in her nose and purple boots.

'Not seen you before, have I?' she asked.

'No, I'm Clo, I'm a friend of Kim's at the pottery,' Clo said, proudly.

'That's cool. Any friend of Kim's is a friend of ours. Hi there, Clo, I'm Angel.'

She handed Clo the bag of carrot cake.

'See you again?'

'Oh yes, I hope so.'

Clo was beginning to feel as though she belonged to this street; her own colourful taste in clothes seemed quite normal among these people. She weighed the odds on Mam allowing her to dye her hair but decided that they were heavily against. She thought how funny it was that, to Mam, it was perfectly OK for Mrs Wilkins to have pink hair, but she would probably think Angel's was shocking.

When she got back the wheelchair was in the shop, but there was no sign of Beth. A hum of voices came from the workshop. Pushing aside the beads Clo was surprised to find her sister sitting at the workbench pounding a lump of clay. Kim worked at the wheel, while Isaac inspected the newly fired pots for cracks. They all seemed to be getting on so well together that for a moment Clo felt like an intruder.

Isaac saw her standing in the doorway. 'Hey there Clo-o-o!' he whooped, 'you come bearing good things, gal?'

Daffy, who had been dozing beneath the bench, was suddenly awake and snuffling round Clo.

'Bones, Daff!' Kim laughed, 'I'm afraid we'll never make a vegetarian out of you. And cake for the workers, I hope?'

Clo held it up.

'Right on, get that kettle boiling.'

Glancing at her watch, Clo was surprised to find that she had been out for nearly an hour and a half.

'Enjoy your walk?' Kim asked.

She nodded.

He moved over to the bench.

'Good, Beth, you're doing well. It's hard working the clay, isn't it, but it'll certainly build up your muscles. Who knows, you may even produce a work of art in the process!'

'I don't think so,' Beth said, 'Clo's the artistic one.'

'You never know,' Kim said.

The shop bell clanged.

'Anyone at home?'

It was Ginny.

'Hi Kim, hi everyone! Oh, goody, just in time for tea by the looks of it, brilliant timing, don't you think?'

Clo thought that you could probably arrive at Aquarius Pots at any time of the day or night and be in time for tea; the kettle was seldom off the boil.

Ginny proceeded to fill them in on the latest horrors they had uncovered at the Manse.

'Wringing damp in the cellar,' she wailed, 'green mould everywhere. It'll have to be seen to. We'll never get moved at this rate and my poor children will have to stay at Camp forever!'

'Really?' Clo asked.

'No, I'm joking, but it's all very inconvenient. So, how are you all getting on?'

'Very well,' Kim said, 'I've told Clo and Beth that they're to come whenever they like. I think we might be able to widen their horizons a little.'

'Good, I thought you might be the right person to do that.'

Clo and Beth looked from Kim to Ginny and back again. There had obviously been some degree of collaboration between them, but they were both too happy to mind.

Kim said, 'My feeling is, we need to get Beth moving independently again. And Clo needs something to stretch her imagination and channel all that energy she's been wasting in frustration.'

It was the first time the situation had been discussed in the hearing of both sisters and they sneaked a look at each other.

'Also time, I think, to be honest with one another about how you feel.'

Ginny nodded. 'Yes, I think you've both been bottling up a lot of difficult feelings about the accident and about being stuck with one another, am I right?'

'Yes,' Clo admitted, 'I certainly have. Sorry, Beth.'

'Me too,' said Beth, to Clo's surprise. 'I know how awful it is for you having to shove me around all day and I haven't really tried to help you. I'm sorry.'

'Very good,' said Ginny. 'No need to blame yourselves for something you can't help, but from now on, try talking to one another, say how you feel, yes?'

She sipped her tea thoughtfully.

'Kim's right, it's high time Beth explored what she can and can't do. I'm sure you've realized he's had plenty of experience in this area.'

'Yes, he's been telling me,' Beth said, 'they expected he would always be in a wheelchair but he was determined he wouldn't—and I feel the same.'

Clo said, 'I'll help you, I promise.'

'Well, that's Beth sorted out,' said Isaac, 'what about Clo?'

Everybody turned to Kim.

'Why are you all looking at me as though I were the oracle?' he said. 'But seeing as you ask, I feel Clo could put her recent experiences to use for the benefit of the community at large.'

Clo's mouth dropped open.

He explained. 'In a very short time you've discovered how user-*un*friendly many public places in Rushworth are to people in wheelchairs...'

'And pushchairs,' Ginny chipped in.

'Quite, and pushchairs, and I think it's high time something was done about it, don't you?'

'The woman in the library said we should complain to the Council,' Clo said.

'She was right, in that the cash to provide access and facilities comes from them, so it's largely a question of making them take it on board as a priority.'

'How do we do that?'

'I think we should begin with our own local councillor—Jim Eccles,' Kim said.

'Do you mean Mr Eccles at the newspaper shop?'

'That's the one.'

'He seems nice, I've been in a few times,' Clo said.

'Do you feel you could go and talk to him about disabled access?' asked Ginny.

'Yes, shall I go now?' Clo was already on her feet.

'Steady on!' Ginny laughed, 'tomorrow will do, best to think it through first. I must go. If you want to come now, girls, I can give you a lift. I'll just get my bag and pay for the plate.'

Kim fetched a scented candle from the shop. He placed it on the workbench, took a box of matches from his pocket and lit it. Nobody said anything but there was a peaceful feeling as the scent of jasmine filled the room.

'I suddenly feel really tired,' Clo said, 'nice tired, though.'

'Me too,' said Beth, closing her eyes.

'I think we've all worked hard this afternoon,' said Kim, 'one way or another. Sometimes just talking can be hard work when it's about something important. Take 'em home, Ginny!'

'With pleasure. Er, Kim, I'm ever so sorry, I've left my purse at home, can I send the money over with Clo?'

'Course,' Kim said. 'Right Clo, Beth, you'll have to come back soon or me and Isaac will be penniless!'

'I was beginning to wonder what had become of you,' Mam said.

'They've been with a friend of mine,' Ginny explained, 'Kim Bell, a potter up Brickfields way.'

'I hope you've not been making a nuisance of yourself, Chloe.'

'No, Mam, he says we can go any time, we're not in the way.'

'Really, Mrs Appleby,' Ginny said, ' he's delighted to let them mess about in the pottery, he's very experienced with youngsters.'

'Well, if you're sure.'

'Absolutely,' Ginny assured her. 'I'm off then, I'll probably pop round tomorrow with that money, Clo, OK? Bye!'

Mam observed Beth's drooping eyelids, 'Eh, you look all in our Beth. Have you been tiring her out, Clo?'

'It's all right Mam, really,' Beth said, 'I've had a lovely day.'

Mam, like Clo, was surprised to hear Beth answering for herself so positively.

'That's all right then. Shall I take you to the bathroom to wash your hands for tea?'

'No thanks, Mam,' Beth said, 'I'll do it by myself, just give me a hand up.'

'Well I never!' said Mam as Beth, holding on to the back of the wheelchair for support, walked slowly out of the room. 'I hope she's not overtaxing herself, I'd better keep an eye on her.'

'Don't worry,' Clo said, 'I think she knows what she's doing and I'll be in the bedroom if she needs me.'

She went out after Beth, as Mam looked on in astonishment.

14

Before they left the flat next day Beth said, 'Clo, can you find me a pair of gloves, please?'

Clo rooted about in the bottom of the wardrobe.

'Only these,' she said, holding up a pair of woollen mittens, 'will they do?'

'They will for now.'

Clo sat on her bed and began to squeeze her feet into her outgrown footwear.

'Ow!' she groaned.

'What's up?'

'They're too small. I think all this extra walking has made my feet grow. I don't want to worry Mam for a new pair, but they're killing me!'

Beth looked concerned. 'Have a look in my sports bag,' she said, 'you can have my trainers, they're no good to me.'

'D'you know where it is?'

'Mam's hidden it somewhere so I can't see it. Try the kitchen cupboard.'

Sure enough, Clo found the bag behind the wellingtons and boxes of old jam jars. She touched the expensive trainers reverently; Beth had won prizes in these. Back in the bedroom she tried them on—they fitted beautifully.

'Thanks, they're smashing, but I don't know what Mam will say.'

'Don't worry, I'll tell her it's all right.'

On their way to Brickfields, Beth suddenly said, 'Stop a minute, I want to try on my own.'

She put on the mittens.

'Kim showed me what to do.'

She began to turn the wheels of the chair with her hands. She managed to get several yards along the pavement before she found herself on a gentle incline and yelled, 'Clo, help!'

Clo dashed after her and caught the handles of the chair. 'That was really good,' she said.

'It's hard work but Kim says I'll get stronger if I practise, it's just like training for a sport.'

'The park would be the best place, it's all on the flat and no traffic. I'll take you over later if you like. I must see Mr Eccles first.'

'Thanks. Have you decided what to ask him?'

'I think so. Doorways and steps and kerbs are the worst, aren't they?'

'Yes, and people thinking you're daft and talking over your head!' Beth said wryly.

So she had noticed, even though she had seemed oblivious to it most of the time.

'You didn't help, just closing your eyes and pretending to be asleep,' Clo said.

'I know, it was easier than getting involved—sorry.'

'Oh, it's OK, I don't blame you. I just used to wish I could do the same.'

'Well I promise I won't do it again,' Beth said, 'from now on, I'm going to answer back! People assume you must be stupid because you're in a wheelchair. Kim says people used to treat him like a halfwit.'

'That's terrible,' Clo said, 'you're still people like everybody else.'

But she cringed as she remembered how embarrassed she had been by the library incident. That was because she'd been thinking of Beth as an albatross instead of a person.

Clo left Beth at the pottery discussing the merits of different types of clay with Kim, and went to see Mr Eccles. She hung about until the shop was empty.

'Please, have you got time to talk about something important?' she asked.

'I reckon so,' Mr Eccles said with a smile, 'it'll be quiet now until dinnertime, come and sit yourself down.'

Clo went round the back of the counter and was given a stool. There were piles of official-looking papers stacked on the floor.

'Council minutes,' he explained, 'I work on them a bit between customers. Now—Chloe, isn't it? What can I do for you?'

'Well, it's about the Council really, you being a councillor and everything. It's you we have to ask when we want something doing, isn't it?'

Mr Eccles looked at her over his spectacles.

'Quite right, young lady. What's on your mind?'

'You know my sister who's in a wheelchair?'

'Yes.'

'Well she's not always been like that, and since I've been looking after her I've—we've had a horrible time, mainly because you can't get wheelchairs up steps, and through doorways that aren't big enough. We think something ought to be done about it because it means lots of people can't do ordinary things like get books out of the library or go shopping.'

'And you are suggesting—what?' Mr Eccles took a pencil from his top pocket.

'At our church we've got a ramp and Kim's got a little one at his shop and that's great. And there is another way into the library, down the side, but you're not allowed to use it and— well, they said I ought to tell the Council,' she finished, breathless.

Mr Eccles wrote a few notes on a paper bag.

'I hear what you're saying,' he said, 'I'm sure it is difficult for people like your sister but the Council only has so much money to spend, and it has to decide what will benefit most of the people.'

'But it's not just people in wheelchairs, it's the people who have to push them. And mums with prams too—there's millions of them!'

'True, true. Go on, you're beginning to convince me.'

'But it's more than that, isn't it? Disabled people are just like you and me. They've got a right to enjoy the same things as us. It's not their fault, it might happen to anybody like it did to Beth.'

'So what you're saying is we need to change people's attitudes?'

'Yes! That's it exactly. So you do agree?'

'Oh yes, I agree with you.'

'So you'll do something about it?'

'Who-a, lass! It's not quite as easy as that. If it was up to me I'd say yes, of course we'll do something, but it isn't, it has to be voted on and adopted as a policy. You'll have to convince the whole Council.'

It was going to be a harder job than Clo had thought but she wasn't going to be put off. 'Right,' she said, 'how do we do that?'

Jim Eccles tapped the side of his nose with his forefinger.

'You need a strategy, a campaign, like. You need petitions, for instance—signatures of people who agree with you, and a demonstration of public opinion, get my meaning?'

'A demonstration?'

'That's right.'

'Will you help?'

'I can't help you demonstrate *as such* but I can make sure the Council takes notice when you do.'

'Thanks,' Clo said. 'I'm not quite sure where to start.'

'Ask that Kim—he looks like he's taken part in a few demonstrations in his time!'

'Right, I will. Thanks ever so much, I'd better go.'

Workers on their dinner hour had started to come into the shop.

'It's a pleasure to be of assistance,' Mr Eccles said, 'after all, that's what your councillors are for. Goodbye. And good luck!'

'He kept talking about demonstrations,' Clo told the others. 'He said you'd know all about those, Kim.'

'I've taken part in a good few marches and protests over the years,' Kim laughed, 'and so has Ginny Lewis—Anti-apartheid, CND, Animal Rights, we've done 'em all! Jim's right, you do have to make people take notice and it takes some organising to put on a successful demo. But I reckon we could do it. We need a steering committee, a group to get things started. Let's have a cup of tea and make some plans.'

While the tea-making was under way Beth said excitedly, 'Kim's going to take me swimming, Clo! He teaches handicapped children to swim.'

'Yes,' Kim said, rummaging among the collection of tea-caddies on the shelf, 'I take some of the children from Whitegates on Monday afternoons, we use the pool at Chorley Fields School—mint tea all right?—Beth told me how much she used to enjoy swimming.'

'Enjoy it?' cried Clo, 'she's a champion—she's won cups and medals for it!'

'She didn't tell me that,' Kim smiled. 'Anyway, swimming is brilliant exercise for getting your strength back so if your grandmother agrees you can both come with me next week.'

'There's no point in me going,' Clo said, 'I'm useless.'

'You know,' Kim said, 'it's good sometimes to do things you don't have a natural aptitude for—like Beth trying to make something with her hands.'

'OK,' Clo said, 'I'll come.'

'Now,' Kim said, 'let's think about this campaign. What else did Jim suggest?'

'A petition.'

'Right, that's something you can begin straight away.'

He handed Clo a sheet of paper and a biro.

'Decide what you want it to say. Begin: We, the undersigned...'

After a few false starts, she wrote:

'We, the undersigned, think it is terrible that people in wheelchairs cannot get up the steps of the library and places like that and we want the Council to do something about it.'

Kim read it. 'It says what you mean but we need to use the sort of language Councils understand. For example, why not put "deplore" instead of "think it's terrible"? Be more assertive—put "demand action" instead of "want something doing"—it shows you mean business.'

'Mmm, OK. Now what?'

'Contact interested parties and call a meeting to plan the campaign.'

'Like who?'

'All the people who have an interest in facilities being improved, and all the people who might be able to help.'

'Right.'

Clo thought for a bit, then made a list:

Disabled People
Babies (in prams)
People who look after both the above
Ernie Earnshaw

'Good start,' Kim said, 'who's Ernie Earnshaw?'

'An old man who showed me the side door at the library. He uses it when he can't get up the steps but he'd get into trouble if they saw him.'

'Of course—old people, pensioners, that's another big group—doesn't your grandmother work at an old people's home?'

'Yes, The Homestead in Moss Farm.'

'Get them involved, then. Howard Lewis would be helpful, vicars know lots of people in the voluntary sector—charities and such like.'

'Will you help?'

'Yes, of course. I know the people at Whitegates and they'll be keen. Then there's every mum with a pushchair in Rushworth—I bet Ginny has contacts with the playgroups.

You've got plenty to be going on with. When will you see Ginny again?'

'Tonight, probably.'

'Right, tell her what we're doing and ask if we can have a planning meeting at the Manse as soon as poss.'

'Will do!' cried Clo, enthusiastically.

'Oh, and you need a slogan. Something like 'Disabled of Rushworth Say, Let Us Come In'—something catchy.'

'Sounds great,' chuckled Beth, 'I think this is going to be fun!'

'Is that you, girls?' Mam called down the stairs, 'wherever have you been? Your tea's been on the table twenty minutes and you know Eric's on lates this week, come on, quick!'

Eric winked at them as he came down for the chair.

Clo helped Beth climb the stairs.

'Sorry, Mam,' she said, running to rinse her hands under the kitchen tap, 'Kim and us are planning a campaign about disabled access and...'

'It's always Kim this and Kim that!' snapped Mam. 'If this Kim had any good sense at all, he'd make sure you got home for your tea on time!'

Beth and Clo caught one another's eyes and silently agreed to postpone any more talk about the campaign until after tea.

When Eric had gone to work Mam said, 'Right, now we can relax, what have you been up to, then?'

Clo said, 'We're campaigning for better access to public buildings, to get the Council to do something about it.'

'Who's "we"?'

'Er, me,' Clo said.

'Well I never!' Mam exclaimed.

'There's other people helping, of course, like Kim and Mr Eccles who's a councillor and Mrs Lewis when I've asked her.'

'You seem to have it all worked out.'

'And there's a petition demanding action, do you think they'd sign it down at The Homestead?'

'Of course they will, or I'll know the reason why. Old people like ours are very limited as to where they can go with their walking frames and chairs.'

'Great!' said Clo. 'We haven't decided what to do for the demonstration yet, we've got to call a meeting.'

'A demonstration, eh? I'm not sure I like the sound of that,' Mam said. 'You mean with banners and shouting and police dogs being called in?'

'I don't know yet. I don't think we need police dogs.'

'Dead right you don't. I shall want to know exactly what you're planning to do, Chloe Olerenshaw.'

'And me,' said Beth.

'Whatever do you mean?'

'I'll be doing it too. After all, it's for the good of people like me.'

Mam shook her head. 'Oh no, Chloe,' she said, 'I'm not having you making a public spectacle of your poor sister.'

'Oh, Mam!' Beth and Clo cried together.

'Mam, it's not like that at all,' Clo said, 'and anyway I don't know what we'll do till after the meeting. Don't worry.'

'We'll see.'

Clearly the subject was closed.

'Mam,' said Beth, 'I want to go swimming, do you know where my costume is?'

Mam was speechless for a minute. Beth might as well have said she wanted to go sky-diving.

'Come again?'

'I want to go swimming,' Beth repeated, 'Kim says he'll take me.'

'Oh no, no, no, that would never do. I'm sorry, lovey, but you're not fit for that sort of thing, you're still far too weak.'

'But Mam, if I don't try I'll never know what I can do and swimming's really good for building you up. Kim's used to taking,'—she hesitated—'disabled people.'

Mam wasn't convinced. 'I don't care,' she said, 'the answer's no and that's the end of it. Clo! Why are you wearing Beth's trainers? You naughty girl, taking advantage like that, we paid good money for those, they're special, not for messing about in!'

'Mam, honestly, I didn't...' Clo began.

'Mam!' Beth interrupted, 'I told Clo to find them and wear them. Her old trainers were hurting her, they're much too small, and let's face it, I've got no use for them.'

Mam began to cry, 'Don't say that, lovey, I can't bear it, of course you will, one day.'

'By then I'll have grown out of them,' Beth said. 'And,' she continued, trembling a little, 'if I don't start doing things for myself and get some proper exercise, I'll never need them again, I'll just stay like this—useless!'

Suddenly the unaccustomed excitement and activity of the

past week caught up with her and she began to sob quietly.

At this point the doorbell rang and Clo escaped to answer it. It was Ginny with the plate money.

Clo whispered, 'I'm glad it's you, Mam's upset because Beth wants to go swimming with Kim and now they're both crying!'

'Oh dear, I do pick my moments!' said Ginny, 'OK, Superwoman is here, what do you want me to say?'

'Just persuade her it's all right for Beth to go swimming, *please*, it means so much to her—oh, and say she needn't worry about the demonstration, either.'

'What demonstration?' Ginny's eyes widened.

'Er, I'll tell you later, just go in,' Clo pleaded.

'Another fine mess you've got me into!' Ginny quipped. She drew a deep breath. 'C'mon Lord, tell me what to say!'

Then, composing herself, she entered the flat with a big smile on her face.

Downstairs Mrs Kawalski opened her door and frowned up the stair well. 'So much noise always!'

'Yes, sorry,' Clo called, 'don't worry, we'll be leaving soon!'

'Too soon it cannot be!' came the reply.

Ginny did her best to reassure Mam. 'Kim's very experienced, Mrs Appleby, he's been teaching children from Whitegates for years. He had polio, you see, and was virtually helpless until somebody took him swimming, and now you'd hardly know.'

'I don't know if the physiotherapist will agree,' Mam said, doubtfully.

'Then let Beth ask her on Friday what she thinks—mention Kim's name, Beth, she's probably heard of him through the grapevine.'

'Thanks, I will,' Beth said, gratefully.

Mam still wasn't completely happy. 'But we don't know anything about this Kim,' she objected, 'I've heard about his shop and the kind of people that go in there!'

'What do you mean?' Clo asked.

Mam tightened her lips. 'Hippies and that. Funny types. Mrs Thorne lives down that way and she told me.'

Clo was furious. 'Honestly, Mrs Thorne's an old—'

'Chloe!' Mam warned.

Ginny said, 'I can vouch for Kim. We were at college together. He may be a bit unconventional, but he's got a heart of 24-carat gold, believe me. I'd trust him with my kids any day.'

105

'Well...'

'Listen,' Ginny said, 'if you like, I'll go too if I can get a sitter for Joel.'

'Fair enough,' Mam said, 'if you'll take responsibility, I'll let her go. I'll admit she's been a lot perkier since they've been going to that pottery, taking more of an interest, like.'

'Yes, *she* has!' said Beth pointedly.

'No need to be cheeky,' Mam said.

'Good, that's settled then.' Ginny got up to go.

'Wait!' Clo cried, 'I've got to tell you all about the campaign. Kim said.'

Ginny sat down again. 'Did you mention a cup of tea, Mrs Appleby?—oh, and if you don't mind, I'd better phone Howard and ask him to put Joel to bed. Looks like I'm here for the duration!'

15

'Ginny says the Manse is too much of a mess but the church hall's free on Friday evening,' Clo told Kim. 'Oh—and here's the money for the plate.'

'Thanks. Yes, Friday's fine by me. Isaac?'

'Cool, man,' Isaac grinned.

'Mr Lewis is going to talk to some people and he said could you speak to Mrs Giddins at Whitegates?'

'Yes, I'll call her tonight. Are you happy to get on with the petition today?'

Clo nodded.

'Can you type?'

He dug out an elderly typewriter from beneath the counter.

'Only with one finger,' Clo said.

'That's plenty! What about you, Beth, what was the verdict on the swimming?'

'Mam wasn't very happy about it,' Beth said, 'but she says I can go if the physiotherapist agrees and Mrs Lewis comes with us.' She made a face. 'Sorry it's so complicated.'

'No, no, your grandmother's only being careful and rightly so,' Kim said, 'after all, she doesn't know me from Adam. Who's your physio?'

'Miss Darnley.'

'No problem, then. I know Miss Darnley.'

'You know everybody!' Clo said.

She blew the dust off the typewriter and painstakingly typed:

'We, the undersigned, deplore the fact that so many public buildings are inaccessible to wheelchair users and people with prams. We demand that the Council does something to remedy this situation and raise public awareness concerning the extra difficulties many disabled people have to endure.'

Ginny and Beth had composed the last bit.

'Yes, I think that has the right ring to it,' Kim said, 'I'll go and get a few more copies done, shan't be long.'

He returned from the printer's with a thick sheaf of paper.

'Goodness, you've done hundreds!' Clo said.

'Well, you'll want to leave quite a few with other people, so keep a list of who has them.'

Clo regarded the pile apprehensively.

'Go to people you know first,' Kim said, 'Mr Eccles, Food for Thought, the butcher—practise on them before you tackle the unknown!'

'Good luck!' Beth called from the workshop.

She was concentrating on building up a bowl with long strips of clay.

'Not bad,' said Mr Eccles, scanning the petition, 'I'll put one on the counter for the customers. Mmm, it reads well—all your own work?'

'The others helped. We're having a meeting in the church hall tomorrow night to plan the demonstration and everything.'

'Good. Now you do understand that I can't get personally involved? But I will tell you this...'

He gave her a few hints before the shop began to fill up.

Clo left him persuading a customer, 'Now, Mrs Smith, I'm sure you'll sympathize with a very good cause and put your name to this petition?'

At Food For Thought Angel said, 'Course we'll take it, we have a special place for petitions, over here.'

She showed Clo a noticeboard behind the door. There were several lists already, for things like saving whales and freeing political prisoners.

'It'll get lost on here,' said Clo, dismayed at how many good causes there were to support.

'No it won't, then, because I'm going to highlight it, see?'

Angel produced a fluorescent felt-tip the same shade as her hair and drew a thick pink line all round the sheet.

'There, they won't miss that,' she said, 'all our regulars look to see what's to be signed. When will you present it?'

'Present what?'

'This, the petition—you have to go and present it to somebody important and get the newspapers there to take photos.'

'Do you?'

'Yeah. That way they can't pretend they haven't received it!'

'Right. I'll mention it at the meeting, thanks.'

'Any time!'

'Good morning, Chloe!' said a voice behind her, 'and what are you up to?'

Turning, Clo saw a very brown pair of legs and followed them up to a pair of red shorts, a white sweatshirt and finally the smiling face of Miss Redmond.

'Hello, Miss! Did you have a nice holiday?'

'Quite breathtaking, thank you. I hope to find an opportunity to show some of my slides next term. How is Elisabeth?'

'Getting better, actually,' Clo said, 'we go to the pottery nearly every day and she likes that. She's going to start swimming again soon.'

'That is good news. I suppose you mean Aquarius Pots down the road? I've never been in but it looks fascinating. And what's all this?' She tapped the petition.

Clo explained.

'That's an excellent idea,' said Miss Redmond. 'If I can be of any help...'

Clo was doubtful. She wasn't sure Miss Redmond was the type to go on demonstrations. 'We're having a meeting tomorrow night. Would you like to come?'

'What time and where?'

Miss Redmond wrote it in her diary.

'You see,' she said, 'I might be able to borrow some equipment from school, a Public Address System for example—loudspeakers for the demonstration, you know?'

'Oh yes! I hadn't thought of that.'

'See you tomorrow, then.'

The butcher's, Busy Needles and Cindy's Fashions all agreed to take petitions and Clo added them to her list.

As she returned to the pottery she met Beth, propelling herself along with more confidence than before.

'Kim says I must practise every day,' she said, 'I'm in training.'

'I saw Miss Redmond in Food for Thought,' Clo said, 'she's been to Turkey. She's coming tomorrow night.'

'A lot of people are interested, aren't they?' said Beth.

'Yes, I've left petitions in five shops. I'm jolly glad I've got your trainers, by the way, my feet think they're in heaven!'

'Yes, they are comfy, aren't they? And they're yours now, remember.'

Clo bent down and hugged her sister.

'Thanks, Beth, I don't know how I could ever have thought of you as an albatross, it was awful of me.'

'A what?' Beth looked baffled.

'Oh, nothing.'

On Friday Clo met Howard Lewis in Rushworth High Street.

'Clo! Glad you've taken this on, how's it going?'

Clo showed him two pages of signatures. 'OK, a bit slow though.'

'Bring some to church on Sunday and I'll talk about it in the service. We'll make them all sign and persuade them to help—delegation, that's the name of the game. You'll have Lizzie and Mary next week, too.'

'Oh good, when?'

'I'm going to fetch them on Monday morning. Pity they'll miss the meeting but I'll fill 'em in on the way home. The more the merrier, eh?'

'Mam took one to The Homestead today, she's having a word with Matron to see what they can do.'

'Good. I've got one or two contacts to follow up. By the way, Clo, would it be helpful if I stage-managed the meeting tonight?'

'Oh, yes, please!'

'See you then, must rush.'

Lillian at Savemore's said, 'I'd like to help, pet, but it just isn't practical on the checkout. What you need is somebody to stand by the door and catch 'em as they go out.'

'Mmm,' said Clo, 'I'll see what I can do.'

She went back outside.

'Peep-peep!' called a cheerful voice, 'nearly ran you over!'

Clo looked up. Mrs Wilkins was being pushed along the pavement by her grandson. She felt suddenly cold inside. So much had happened in the last few days, she had forgotten that she had to avoid Mrs Wilkins.

'It's Mabel Appleby's granddaughter, isn't it?'

Mrs Wilkins peered through her thick spectacles.

'Pull over a minute, Mark!' she ordered, 'I want a word with this lass!'

Mark put the brake on and wandered off to look in the cycle shop.

Clo's heart sank; now she was for it.

'Now then,' Mrs Wilkins said, 'your granny tells me that you're having a campaign about getting into places with wheelchairs, right?'

'Yes.'

'I hadn't realized you were Beth's sister, by the way. I haven't seen her lately but Mabel says she's improving no end.'

She obviously hadn't connected the incident outside the Library with Beth at all; she was too short-sighted to recognize anybody unless they were close up.

'You're a good girl,' she continued, 'and I wanted to tell you that if there's anything I can do, you're to say. I may be an old woman but I'm not finished yet.'

Clo knew exactly how she could help: 'Actually there is something, something very important. You like sitting by the checkout at Savemore's watching what's going on, don't you?'

'Ooh I do, my duckie, see all my friends that way.'

'We've got this petition, you see. How would you like to have a copy of it and get everyone to sign it as they come out?'

'Course I will! I won't let them by till they sign, don't you worry!'

'Lillian says she's sure it'll be all right.'

'It'd better be—my son's the manager!' chuckled Mrs Wilkins. 'Give it here, duck, and I'll start tomorrow.'

'Thanks, it will be better coming from you because you're... well, you're affected by it.'

'Dead right I am, though I'm luckier than most. I'm hoping to get one of those little motorized chairs soon, so I can run around on my own. I can't wait!'

Clo couldn't help thinking that a motorized Mrs Wilkins might be something of a hazard but she said, 'That'll be great, Mrs Wilkins, thanks, bye!'

Another problem solved. She found herself outside the Sari Shop and stopped to look. As she was feasting her eyes Mr Rashid came to the door.

'My friend Chloe!' he greeted her, 'we have not seen you for so long, why did you run away last time? We are so sorry for your sister, how is she?'

'Better, thanks. Sorry I didn't stop before.'

'And you are collecting names to present to the Council, I hear?'

'Goodness,' thought Clo, 'news travels fast!'

'Come in and explain it to us,' Mr Rashid said, 'my wife will like to see you.'

Clo stepped into the exotic atmosphere of bright silks, gauzy scarves and the now-familiar perfume. Patchouli, Kim said it was.

'Coo-ee, welcome!'

Mrs Rashid detached herself from a group of women fingering materials at the counter and came over.

Mr Rashid spoke quickly to her in Gujerati, indicating Clo and the papers she carried.

Mrs Rashid nodded gravely, then said in careful English, 'We will help you if we can, we care very much about such things.'

'Do you?' Clo was surprised.

Mr Rashid smiled sadly, 'Oh yes, Chloe. You have never met Abdul, have you, our little boy?'

'No, I don't think so.'

'Come.' Mrs Rashid beckoned her to the back of the shop where she drew aside a bead curtain like Kim's.

In the living quarters behind sat a tiny figure in a heavily padded wheelchair far bigger than himself. He was looking at a picture book, turning the pages with twisted little hands and making small sounds to himself.

'This is Abdul,' said Mrs Rashid, stroking his hair.

'Oh.' Clo was shocked. 'I didn't know.'

'He is our son, we love him,' Mrs Rashid said simply, 'but we wish we could do more for him.'

'He is at a special boarding school most of the time,' Mr Rashid explained, 'but in the holidays there is not much to interest him. As you say so rightly, many places are not accessible.'

'It's for people like him,' said Clo, 'that we're having this campaign. Will you have a copy of the petition on the counter and ask your customers to sign it?'

'Certainly, but is that all?' asked Mr Rashid.

'We're hoping to have a big demonstration and a march to make people notice, but I don't know when yet.'

'Please tell us as soon as you know, the Asian community also has a voice, we also have our disabled and infirm. We will do anything we can.'

He opened the till and took out five ten-pound notes.

'Here. You will need funds to get things moving.'

'Goodness! Thank you,' said Clo, 'I expect we will.'

She stowed the money safely away.

'I'll let you know what happens. And my friend Ginny wants to come and meet you. I showed her some bits of silk you once gave me and she loved them. She might even buy a sari!'

'We shall be honoured to supply her, and my wife will be pleased to assist her with it,' said Mr Rashid graciously.

The ambulance had just dropped Beth off as Clo rounded the corner of Raglan Street.

'Sorry I'm late,' she panted, 'I was telling Mr and Mrs Rashid about the campaign—did you know they've got a son who's disabled?—I forgot the time.'

'Clo!' Beth couldn't wait to tell her. 'Miss Darnley says there couldn't be anything better for me than swimming. She knows Kim and thinks he's marvellous!'

Clo grinned. Everything was beginning to fall into place.

'That's great,' she said, 'Mam will never be able to say no now!'

16

By 6.30 pm Clo was becoming agitated. Tea was cleared away but Mam refused to rush. 'Stop fidgeting, Clo,' she said, 'we'll be there by seven, it's only ten minutes' walk.'

'You know, you don't really have to come,' Clo said.

'Oh yes I do!' Mam retorted. 'I want to know what you're up to!'

Clo knew it was useless arguing when Mam had made her mind up.

'Did you take the petition to work?' she asked.

'Yes, I meant to say. Matron thinks it's a very good idea but she doesn't feel she can do anything because she's leaving. Apparently her mother's ill and she's off to Scotland at the end of the month. We had no idea.'

'Oh.' Clo was disappointed.

'Don't fret, lovey,' said Mam, taking her pinny off, 'I'll do what I can, Matron's perfectly happy for me to organize something.'

'Thanks, now *please*—hurry!'

Howard was welcoming people at the door of the church hall.

'Hang on a minute,' he said, 'I'll get some help to carry Beth downstairs.'

'No,' Beth said, 'I'll get down on my own, on my bottom if necessary.'

'But you'll get all mucky!' Mam protested.

'Don't let Mrs Thorne hear you say that,' laughed Howard, 'she swept those stairs this morning!'

Kim was waiting at the bottom to give Beth a hand up.

'Mam, this is Kim,' Clo introduced them.

Mam's eyes widened as she took in Kim's pony-tail, earrings and Doc Marten boots. Clearly he confirmed all her worst suspicions.

But he disarmed her by saying, 'Mrs Appleby, I'm very pleased to meet you, let me find you a comfortable seat.'

A circle of chairs was set out in the hall. Apart from Mam and the girls there were Ginny and Howard, Kim, Isaac,

Miss Redmond and Mrs Giddins from Whitegates.

Howard stood up. 'Welcome everybody,' he said, 'it's a great pleasure to host the inaugural meeting...'

'The *what*?' Clo whispered to Ginny.

'The first,' Ginny whispered back.

'... the inaugural meeting of such an important campaign, and not before time, by all accounts.'

'Hear, hear!' said Mrs Giddins.

'First of all,' said Howard, 'I would like to call on Chloe Olerenshaw who is heading up this initiative to tell us how she came to have the idea. Clo.'

He sat down.

Everyone waited expectantly for Clo to speak.

'Er... I... ahem.' She coughed.

'Take your time,' Howard said, 'we're all friends here.'

Clo smiled nervously. 'Thanks.'

Once she started it was easy; she recounted some of the difficulties and prejudices she had come up against in the past few weeks, how frustrating it had been for her, as well as Beth, not to be able to do very ordinary things, and how trapped she had felt.

Mam looked down at her hands in the same way Clo did when she thought she was being told off, and Ginny reached over and patted her arm.

Then Beth told her side of it, how some people's ignorance and others' protectiveness had made her feel helpless and so depressed that in the end she had just withdrawn into herself. But then she had met Kim who had been through the same sort of experience, and now she was determined to stand up for herself and for other disabled people.

Mam said, 'Oh dear, I can't do anything right. I only did what I thought was best.'

'Now, Mrs Appleby, none of that,' said Howard firmly, 'you did your best in very difficult circumstances. You must not, repeat not, blame yourself.'

'Oh no, Mam, you mustn't,' said Clo, 'you've always done everything for us, we don't want you any different.'

Mam blew her nose and managed a smile.

'Right,' Howard said, 'I think we all appreciate what we are up against: one, lack of proper access to public facilities and two, sheer ignorance. Clo has begun to distribute a petition— would you like to read it to us, Clo?'

Clo read it out to murmurs of approval.

'Now,' said Howard, 'can I take suggestions from the floor for furthering the campaign, to culminate in a suitable demonstration which will attract the right kind of publicity?'

'Culmi-what?' whispered Clo.

'End up with,' Ginny whispered back, 'don't worry, it's only committee-speak!'

'I heard that!' said Howard.

'Just translating, dear!' said Ginny. 'As you say, we need something that will attract people's attention. I feel it ought to be on a Saturday when lots of people are about, and before the end of the school holidays. That means we only have three weeks, not long.'

Kim agreed. 'Yes, we'll have to move fast so we should be aiming for simplicity with maximum impact—do you remember the CND demos, Ginny, when we all used to turn up in boiler suits and gas masks and lie down in the road pretending to be nuclear victims?'

Ginny giggled. 'Yes, we painted round our shapes—and we got summonsed for criminal damage because they couldn't get the paint off!'

Mam looked disapproving.

'Hmm, not quite appropriate in this case,' Howard said, 'but something similar.'

'Personally,' said Mrs Giddins, 'I favour the presence of as many wheelchair users as we can muster, make visible the people who are usually made to feel invisible. I could bring several dozen disabled youngsters and their helpers.'

'And we can bring about ten old people from the Home if we can find folks willing to push them,' said Mam.

'Good. Now all we need is a time and place. Clo?' Howard turned to her.

Clo did some calculations. 'It will have to be Saturday the 4th,' she said. 'Morning's the busiest time so how about 10.30?'

'Fine,' said Howard, 'where?'

Everybody thought.

Then Beth said, 'Perhaps it ought to be somewhere wheelchair users find a problem, in order to make it obvious. I vote for Rushworth Library.'

'Gosh, the Dragon will be furious!' giggled Clo.

'Breathing fire at the very least!' said Howard, 'but she won't be able to object. In front of the steps is a public right of way. We will, of course, have to get permission.'

'Who from?' somebody asked.

116

'The police,' Ginny said, 'any march or demo needs to be cleared with the police.'

'Oh dear,' murmured Mam.

'But if they approve, and I'm sure they *will* approve a peaceable demonstration like this, they give you an escort through the traffic, which is a great help.'

'We need to get onto that immediately,' said Howard, 'who'll take it on?'

'I think you should,' said Isaac, 'just flash your dog-collar—they're bound to think it's OK!'

'All right, I'll do it!' said Howard. 'So: as many elderly and disabled people in wheelchairs as we can get plus helpers...'

'Ahem!' Ginny was trying to get a word in edgeways.

'I know just what you're going to say, my love—mums with babies. We've got a list of playgroups and things haven't we?'

'Yes, I'll phone all the leaders as soon as poss. We'll jam the High Street with pushchairs and screaming kids!'

'Good,' said Howard, 'now what are we going to do to make it attractive? I know it's a serious subject but...'

'But we don't want to put people off,' said Mrs Giddins, 'it needs a light touch, I feel...'

'A party atmosphere,' put in Miss Redmond, 'bright, amusing, music, all that sort of thing...'

'Yeah—car-nee-val!' whooped Isaac. 'Some guys I know play in a jazz band and I know some steel drummers too, want them?'

'Oh yes, that sounds wonderful,' said Clo. 'Shall we dress up?' she asked, hopefully.

'Why not?' everyone said. 'What as?'

'What about clowns?' suggested Miss Redmond, 'it's easy enough to paint faces and make a few ruffles, and it means everybody can join in, even in wheelchairs.'

'Brilliant!' enthused Ginny, 'I like it.'

This was voted unanimously.

'I'll organize that,' said Miss Redmond, 'I can get some people from my drama group to help with the make-up. We'll need a rallying point to get people ready on the day.'

'Mmm,' Howard said, 'we're not really close enough here—but I know Father Dennis at St Joseph's and their hall is near the library. Leave it to me.'

'Now all we need is a slogan,' Kim said, 'and a poster to put it on.'

'OK,' said Howard, 'let's brainstorm. Just say whatever comes into your head, and we'll see what we end up with.'

'Something about not being able to get inside,' Beth began, 'like, Don't Leave Us Out In The Cold—that sort of thing.'

'Don't Lock Us Out,' Clo suggested.

'Use the clown theme?' said Miss Redmond, 'It's No Laughing Matter When You Can't Get In?'

'Open Up And Let Us In!' roared Isaac.

Howard was rapidly taking notes.

'I like Open Up,' he said, 'it's snappy. How about the Open Up Campaign? We can supplement it with banners on the day explaining a bit more—especially the No Laughing Matter, I like that.'

Kim nodded. 'Yes. I'll draft the poster if you like. Trouble is, they'll be a bit pricey to print.'

Clo felt in her pocket. 'Will £50 pay for them?'

'Yes, I think my friend Tom down the Printshop could do a good job for £50,' Kim said, 'why?'

'Because that's how much we've got!' cried Clo, triumphantly producing the money.

Mam looked alarmed. 'Wherever did you get all that money?'

'Mr Rashid gave it me,' said Clo and she explained about Abdul and how Mr Rashid wanted to get the people in his community involved.

'Absolutely splendid!' said Mrs Giddins, 'Good man! What an example!'

'Brilliant,' said Howard, 'things are moving. Can we get those posters out next week, do you think?'

'Sure,' Kim said. 'I'll ask Tom for a nice bright colour too.'

'Well, I think we've done enough for one evening,' Howard said. 'Same time next week OK, everybody?'

This was pencilled into diaries.

On the way out Howard said to Clo. 'Hope I didn't take the show over—are you happy with everything?'

'I *think* so. There's only one thing worrying me.'

'What's that?'

'Well, we know where we're meeting on the day and what we're doing but where are we marching to?'

'Good question. Wherever we present the petition, I suppose. Maybe you should pop over and have a word in your Mr Eccles' ear. He'll know.'

On Saturday Clo did the shopping as usual. True to her word Mrs Wilkins was sitting in the sunshine outside the supermarket with the petition.

'How are you getting on?' Clo asked.

'First rate my duckie!' was the answer, 'look at all these names! Got any spare sheets? I'll need 'em.'

Clo fished some out of the shopping trolley.

'Thanks duckie, that's lovely. Oi, Albert Parker!' she shouted at an old man shuffling out of the door, 'come here, I want a word with you!'

Mrs Wilkins certainly wasn't letting anybody slip past her!

Clo hurried home and dumped the shopping on the kitchen table.

'Here it is Mam, must dash, got to see Mr Eccles.'

'Stay where you are young lady! You'll have something to eat first. You need to keep your strength up for this campaign.'

'Oh... all right.' Clo sat down.

She looked round. 'Where's Beth?'

'Down the street, practising in her chair. She's very determined, I'll say that for her. I'd never have believed it a few weeks ago.'

She cut the bread and looked sideways at Clo.

'You two seem to be getting on a bit better as well.'

'Yes,' Clo admitted, 'it was a lot easier after Ginny and Kim made us talk to each other!'

Mr Eccles had a large basket over his shoulder and was locking his shop door.

'Mr Eccles, don't go! I need to ask you something!' Clo panted.

'You just caught me,' he said, 'I'm off for an afternoon's fishing—what's your problem?'

'We've planned the demonstration and everything, but we need to know who to take the petition to, and where.'

'That's easy, you take it to the Town Hall, of course. When is it?'

Clo told him.

'Right, leave it with me. If I can get somebody important to receive it, I will, if not, I'll do it myself. And make sure you let the newspapers know.'

'We will, thanks. We'll have the posters next week, will you put one up for us?'

'Of course. By the way, have you got another copy of that petition? Ours is nearly full.'

'Yes!'

Clo whipped one out of her bag and Mr Eccles posted it through his own letter-box.

'You're doing well Chloe,' he said, 'have you written your speech yet?'

Clo gaped at him. 'What speech?'

'You have to start the proceedings with a speech, a real rouser that gets everybody going. Then, hopefully, they'll follow you down the Town Hall. The bigger the crowd, the more impact you'll make, see?'

'Oh gosh, I didn't know that. Oh dear!'

'Don't worry, lass,' said Mr Eccles cheerfully, shouldering his fishing tackle, 'you've got three whole weeks to think on it—ta-ta now.'

Clo was left quaking at the prospect. She, Chloe Olerenshaw, make a speech? She hadn't expected that! She went straight to Aquarius Pots and told Kim.

'Quite right,' Kim said, concentrating on fixing a handle to a teapot, 'don't worry.'

'But I *am* worried!'

'Don't be,' Kim repeated, 'you don't need to do it all yourself. It's better if people speak for themselves, all you need do is give an introduction then call on one or two other people to speak from their own point of view. Your Mrs Wilkins might be one—she sounds pretty fearless!— and someone representing an organization, like Mrs Giddins.'

'I bet Ernie Earnshaw would if I can find him,' Clo said.

'That's right. Ask Mr Rashid too. The thing to aim for is to let folks see that people of all ages and conditions are affected by lack of access, do you see?'

'Yes. Thanks.'

Clo's eyes strayed along the workbench.

'Oh, that's nice,' she said, pointing to a round pot about six inches high with birds scratched into its surface.

'Beth made it.'

'Really?' Clo was amazed; Beth had never been interested in making things before.

'Yes, really. Good, isn't it? She worked really hard on it. The decoration is simple but effective. It should look good when it's fired.'

'I'd like to have a go, sometime,' said Clo, wistfully.

'So you shall,' smiled Kim, 'when you've got a minute from

organizing campaigns! Seriously though, I run a Saturday class in the winter; come to that, I think you'd enjoy it.'

'OK.'

'Have a look on the drawing board, I've started the poster.'

He had drawn a stylized group of people in wheelchairs, on crutches and frames and in pushchairs, all reaching out and knocking on a barred door.

The lettering said,

'OPEN UP! CAMPAIGN FOR ACCESS TO PUBLIC PLACES IN RUSHWORTH. BIG DEMONSTRATION AND CELEBRATION 4TH SEPTEMBER 10.30 A.M., LIBRARY SQUARE'.

'It's great,' Clo said, 'but will people know we mean the bit in front of the library steps?'

'What with Isaac's steel band and hundreds of clowns, I don't think they'll be able to miss it! By the way, your Miss Redmond came in this morning, I'm sure she'd help with the speech. I took up her offer of the school PA system as well, OK?'

'Yes, we'll need that. Did she like everything—the shop, I mean?'

'She seemed suitably impressed. She bought two packets of joss-sticks, a stoneware colander and some wind-chimes. Oh and she ordered a two-pint teapot—this!'

He waved the teapot he was working on.

'Gosh,' said Clo, 'I never thought of Miss Redmond as a joss-stick type of person.'

'You can't always go by appearances. She told me all about her trip to Turkey—maybe that's what did it—plus the jasmine tea! Want a cup?'

Clo spent the afternoon out with the petition accompanied by Daffy, who waited patiently outside shops while she went inside. Finally they drifted into the park and sat in the sunshine beside the lake.

'No more hiding in the shadows for me, Daff,' Clo said, stretching in the sun, 'it's a lot better out in the open.'

She ruffled the little dog's coarse fur.

'It was you who came and found me, Daffy, when I was really miserable and couldn't believe that things could ever get better—I think you were one of those little presents Ginny talks about. And you know, it's funny, even though things haven't really changed—we still haven't got anywhere to live and Beth's still not better—it's different just because we're

121

doing something about it. Are you sure you're not my guardian angel in disguise?'

Daffy reached up and licked her face.

Clo could have sworn he was grinning at her, as if to say, 'Could be. What do *you* think?'

17

All weekend Clo worried about the speech. She couldn't help it; whatever she happened to be doing it niggled away at the back of her mind.

Mam laughed when she mentioned it. 'What,' she said, 'you, frightened of saying a few words in public? Remember the play—you didn't have any trouble then, did you?'

But that had been different somehow.

Beth was woken early Monday morning by anguished moans coming from Clo's bed. She reached over and shook her.

'Clo, are you ill?'

Clo peered at her, bleary-eyed. 'What?'

'You sounded as if you were in pain.'

'No, really, I'm fine. I was dreaming about the demonstration. I was standing on the Town Hall steps and all these reporters were holding microphones out—like they do on telly—and I couldn't think of a single word to say, I just froze. Then everybody started booing and throwing things at me. It was horrible!'

'You need some tips from an expert,' Beth said.

'You're right. In fact Kim did suggest I ask Miss Redmond.'

'Well, do it then. Ring her up.'

'All right. What time is it?'

'Six o'clock, a bit early for making phone calls! Better get some more sleep.'

Clo buried her head in her pillow and was fast asleep in seconds. But Beth lay awake, watching the sun grow brighter beyond the bedroom curtains, and thinking about swimming.

As soon as Mam had left for work Clo reached for the telephone directory, and looked up the only D. Redmond in the book.

'Can't have you moaning and groaning all night long, I need my sleep!' said Beth.

Clo dialled the number.

'Diana Redmond here, hello?'

'Oh. Oh, it's Chloe, Miss Redmond. It's about the speech I've got to give at the demo. I'm really worried about it.'

'Are you responsible for the whole thing?'

'No, only the introduction, the rest's to be people from the different groups.'

'Right, then your job is to give the crowd information: who you represent, why you are all assembled, and where you are marching to—any idea where that will be?'

'Yes, the Town Hall to give in the petition.'

'Make that clear at the beginning. Then introduce the other speakers with, "Now so-and-so from Whitegates—or whatever—would like to say a few words"—something like that. At the end sum up and invite people to join the march. How does that sound?'

'That's great, Miss, I think I can do that.'

'I'm sure you can, Chloe. Write down what you want to say, you can use notes on the day, that's perfectly acceptable. We'll have a rehearsal nearer the time.'

'Thanks, Miss, I've been having nightmares about it!'

'Poor Chloe! Don't lose any sleep, it'll be fine, you'll see,' Miss Redmond assured her.

Clo replaced the receiver, a weight off her mind. She got out an old jotter, wrote, 'Who? Why? Where?' Before she knew it Ginny had arrived to take them to the swimming pool.

'Sorry I'm late,' she said, 'it's complete chaos at our house, what with the girls coming home today and everything half-packed to move. Then on top of that the babysitter got held up. Talk about "the best laid schemes"!'

She bundled the wheelchair into the boot while Clo helped Beth into the car.

'Do you know when you're moving yet?' Beth asked.

'Goodness only knows. The Wreck just seems to develop one nasty problem after another—it's woodworm in the floorboards, now. Still, mustn't grumble, we do have a roof over our heads. Any sign of a place for you?'

'No, nothing yet,' said Clo.

'Don't lose heart,' Ginny said, 'God's timing is perfect and somewhere he's got the perfect place for you. Oops, sorry!' She braked suddenly at some traffic lights. 'I rang round all the playgroup leaders yesterday and most of them were keen to get involved. Someone suggested balloons with the Open Up slogan on for the kiddies.'

'Good idea,' said Clo, 'I'll ask Kim. Lots of people signed up at church yesterday, didn't they?'

'Mmm, Howard certainly laid it on pretty thick, saying it was their Christian duty to get involved in human rights issues! Even Mrs Thorne signed and said she'd bring her Auntie Annie to the demo!'

At Chorley Fields School a minibus with 'Whitegates' on the side was unloading half a dozen youngsters with the help of a hydraulic lift built into the back.

Kim popped his head out, 'Hi there! You go on through and get changed, we'll be with you in a couple of shakes, won't we, Gary?'

He was helping a boy in a chair onto the lift. The boy waved jerkily at them and laughed. Beth got into her chair and propelled herself across the yard and up the ramp into the sports hall without looking back.

'This is a big step for her,' Ginny said, and Clo nodded.

Each child had someone who helped them change and reach the pool. Beth, however, insisted on doing everything herself and was soon sitting on the edge, looking apprehensively into the water.

'Are you OK?' Clo asked.

'Mmm.' She seemed a little unsure.

The other children obviously enjoyed their swimming lessons immensely and shrieked with laughter as they were helped in. Gary waved and shouted something that Clo couldn't quite catch.

'He says, "come on in, it's lovely!" ' interpreted Jane, his helper, and Gary nodded vigorously. Kim swam over. He limped quite badly with his leg brace off, but he swam like a fish.

'Well, Beth,' he said quietly, 'ready to give it a try?'

Beth nodded, and Clo and Kim helped her into the water where she stood shivering for a moment or two.

'OK?' Kim asked.

'Yes, I am, really,' she said, 'it's just so strange being here with all these others and knowing that I'm... one of them. I'm a disabled person too.'

'It's not a matter of "them" and "us", Beth,' Kim said gently, 'in a sense, we're all "them" and we're all "us". We're all human beings with difficulties and abilities. I've got a gammy leg but I can make good pots; Gary's got cerebral palsy but he knows more about computers than you or I will ever know! We're all a bit different, that's all, and some of us need more help than others. There's no shame in that.'

Beth nodded. 'Even if I never do those things I used to again, there'll be other things I can do just as well.'

'You've got it,' Kim said, 'now how about a gentle swim up the side?'

Beth submerged her shoulders and grinned. Then she stretched out her arms, kicked her legs and began to swim.

'I'll keep an eye on her,' Ginny said.

Kim moved off to help the others. 'Give us a hand, Clo?' he called.

Clo followed eagerly. The children's pleasure was infectious and she wanted to join in the fun.

Beth swam steadily, enjoying the warmth of the water and the weightlessness of her body. She reached the far end, turned expertly, and swam back down.

'Good?' Ginny asked.

'Yes, it feels lovely. I can still do it, I know I can!'

She plunged back, changing to a stylish crawl. Minutes later she was holding on to the side, gasping for breath.

'I... thought... I thought I could still do it,' she said, nearly in tears, 'but I can't!'

'Of course you can,' Ginny said, 'you've just swum six lengths when you've scarcely walked anywhere for months. I can't swim that far! Beth, you're doing brilliantly.'

'But this is pathetic!' Beth wailed.

'Now listen to me, Elisabeth Olerenshaw, you only think that because you're used to being a champion and winning medals all over the place, unlike us ordinary mortals. Look at those kids over there. It'll be a major achievement if any one of them ever does what you've just done, so stop feeling sorry for yourself! Keep on as you are and it won't be long before you're winning races again. Don't lose heart, Beth, please.'

'Sorry, you're right—it's just so frustrating.'

Ginny hugged her. 'I know,' she said.

'That was great, Beth,' Kim said, 'it won't take long to get you back in shape. OK, forget the Olympic performance and just relax.'

Beth did as she was told and floated gently on her back for the rest of the session.

Afterwards he said, 'Well done, Beth, you've taken a bigger step on the road to recovery today than you realize. You *will* recover, you know. And I think even Clo enjoyed herself, didn't you, Clo?'

Clo had to admit she had. 'Gary's really funny,' she said, 'I could understand what he was saying after a while—he was telling me all these terrible jokes!'

'Yes, our Gary's quite a comedian! I'm off to collect the posters now. See you both tomorrow.'

As they drove back through Chorley Fields Ginny said, 'Fancy calling at our house before I take you home? Howard may have some more information about the demo.'

'But he's gone to Brinkley, hasn't he?' asked Clo.

'Been and...'

She swerved round into Sycamore Avenue,

'... come back, by the looks of things.'

She parked untidily behind her husband's car.

Clo's eyes lit up. 'So Lizzie and Mary are... ?'

'Mum!' Lizzie threw herself out of the front door. 'Mummy! And Clo and Beth!—hey, Mary, Clo and Beth are here too!'

They both hugged and squeezed Ginny and Clo but they hung back a little from Beth, not quite knowing how to treat her.

But Beth eased herself out of the car, held out her hand and said, 'Hello, we've never really met properly, I'm Beth.'

Clo saw the look of surprise which passed between Lizzie and Mary; Beth had changed almost beyond belief in two weeks.

Howard came out with Joel. 'Enjoy your swim, you lot?'

'I'll be stiff as a board tomorrow,' groaned Ginny. 'Beth put us all to shame, didn't she, Clo?'

'Oh yes, but then she's a *real* swimmer.'

Beth looked pleased. 'I'm a bit rusty but I'll get back into it.'

There was much hilarity over tea as they all recounted the activities of the past few weeks: 'We had a midnight raid on the Main Street Methodist lot—we pulled their tent pegs out,' laughed Mary, 'they didn't know what'd hit them!'

'I'd love to have seen it,' Clo gasped, 'isn't Derek Gibson one of their lot?'

'Yes, he tried to escape but we got him with a bucket of water!'

'What a bunch of little angels!' said Howard.

'Did you really sneak into the library in disguise, Clo?' asked Lizzie, 'ooh, I wish I'd been there! It'll serve the old Dragon right when we demonstrate, she will be mad. We *can* join in, can't we?'

'Of course, there's lots to do if you'll help.'

'Course we will,' said Mary, 'we had clowns at Camp and I've learnt to juggle a bit, can I do that on the day?'

'Brilliant!' Clo cried, 'oh yes, anything like that. Will you help with the posters tomorrow?'

'Yes, yes!' yelled Lizzie, and Joel screamed with delight.

'Enough! Calm down, you lot,' shouted Ginny, 'I can't hear myself think! Now girls, Daddy's probably explained to you that our moving plans have been scuppered yet again and everything is in a frightful muddle? So yes, please get involved in this campaign. As Clo says, there's lots to do. Not that I want to drive you out of the house, my dear children, but...'

'But you'd like us out of the way. OK, OK!' laughed Mary, 'don't worry, we'll make ourselves scarce!'

When they got home Mam and Eric had only just got in themselves. They seemed excited about something.

'Where have you been?' Clo asked.

'Er, only to look at a place we might be moving to,' said Eric.

'Where is it?' Clo and Beth wanted to know.

'Um... er, not far,' Mam said.

'Is it nice? Is it a flat or a proper house? Has it got a garden?'

'Er, yes, it's nice and it's... a house,' Eric said, cautiously.

'Wonderful! When are we moving?' Clo demanded.

'Nothing's settled,' Mam said, 'so don't go setting your heart on it because it might come to nothing. There'll have to be an interview.'

'What do you mean, an interview?' asked Beth.

'With the proper people. To see if it would suit... er, everybody,' she said mysteriously. 'As I say, don't count on it. Now, how was your swimming? Did you dry yourselves properly? Your hair looks damp still, Clo, better get a towel to it. Beth?'

Beth grinned. 'It was really good. I can still swim and I'll improve. It was a good idea of Kim's.'

'You look tired,' Mam said, anxiously.

'I'm absolutely shattered!' said Beth, 'but I feel great.'

'That's marvellous, lovey. There's a note for you, by the way.'

She handed Beth a folded piece of paper.

'It's from Jenny and Janice,' Beth said, 'they've heard

about the demo and they want to help.'

'We could do with some strong youngsters to push the old folks,' said Mam.

'I'm sure they'd do that,' Beth said, 'I'll ring Jenny now.'

She got up and, holding on to the furniture as she went, walked out to the hall.

'I'd never have believed the difference in her,' whispered Mam to Eric, 'it's an answer to prayer and no mistake.'

18

They all converged on the pottery next morning; Clo and Beth arrived under their own steam and the Lewises dropped off Lizzie and Mary on their way to the Wreck.

'Hi there you two!' Kim greeted the Lewis girls, 'survived blowy Brinkley, then?'

'Oh, do you know each other?' Clo asked, surprised. She had been looking forward to introducing her friends to one another.

'Know 'em?' laughed Kim, 'I remember them when they were dribbling down their bibs! Nice to have you both on board. Just in time too—we've got fifty posters and several hundred leaflets to get rid of, all in fluorescent orange—ta-ra!'

He unrolled a poster with a flourish. They all blinked.

'Goodness, where are my sunglasses?' said Ginny, 'that's quite... er...'

'Appalling?' Kim suggested. 'Tom got it cheap—you can see why—but it means we get more for our money.'

'I don't think anybody's going to miss that,' said Lizzie, squinting.

'Yuk no!' said Mary.

'So much the better,' said Howard, 'you can't afford to be subtle with publicity, you want people to notice it.'

Isaac came through wiping clay off his hands. 'Hey, that's cool,' he said, admiringly, 'great colour, man!'

'Cool wouldn't be the word I'd use for it,' said Kim.

'I like it too,' said Clo, 'it sort of sizzles at you.'

The shop bell rang and a lady in a straw hat peeped nervously round the door.

'Is it all right to come in?' she asked, timidly.

Kim helped her squeeze through.

'Come in, Mrs Avery,' he said, 'we're a bit crowded, sorry. It's all to do with the Open Up Campaign.'

He showed her the poster.

Mrs Avery shaded her eyes with her hand to read it.

'What an excellent idea, Mr Bell. If you can spare one I'll take it along to the Mothers' Union at St Peter's, they'll be very interested.'

'Please do,' Howard said, 'they're just the sort of organization we want involved.'

'If there's anything I can do to help... ?'

'That's a dangerous thing to say around here!' said Kim. 'Don't you run a banner-making group at your church?'

'Yes I do, what had you in mind?'

'Something large but fairly simple to head up a procession. Would there be time to make one?'

'I don't see why not.'

'Wait till I've cleared this lot out,' said Kim, 'and I'll do a sketch for you. Phew! I think we're going to have to find a campaign office somewhere now things are hotting up. We could do with a phone as well.'

'Right, we'll transfer operations to the church hall,' Howard said, 'there's plenty of room there. I'll sort it out straight away.'

Ginny rolled her eyes. 'I have a nasty feeling we're not going to get any more decorating done until this campaign is over—bye-ee!'

The girls distributed quite a lot of posters round Brickfields.

'But we need to spread them further,' Clo said.

Kim produced a street map.

'Divide that up so that posters go to every area of Rushworth. But remember, we've got a meeting on Friday and we can ask the others to take some. No need to wear yourselves out.'

'What happened with the banner lady?' Beth asked.

'Good news. Mrs Avery has offered to sew us a proper banner with Open Up Rushworth on it. I've seen some of her church banners and she's a genius. But you'll still need plenty of placards for people to carry. You'll also need to draw a map of the route to photocopy and send to all the groups taking part. Mary, you're good at maps, aren't you?'

'Yes, I can do that,' Mary said.

'What if we start on the placards this afternoon?' suggested Clo.

'Sounds good,' said Kim. 'Ask round the shops for cardboard boxes—in fact, it's market day today, if you hurry you'll be able to get the boxes and stuff before the dustcart comes for them. I'll lend you Isaac and the van.'

Mary and Beth decided to go straight to the church hall and get on with the paperwork. Beth carried Kim's battered typewriter on her lap and Mary pushed. Clo and Lizzie got ready to leave for the market.

'It's getting like Rushworth Railway Station round here, man!' said Isaac, 'and it used to be so nice and peaceful.'

Kim laughed. 'And it will be again when all this is over, don't worry.'

'I'm not complaining,' said Isaac. 'My mates in the band are dead keen, by the way, and even my mum says what can she do to help?'

'Ask her to come on Friday,' Kim said, 'she's a dressmaker, isn't she? I bet we can find her something to do. See you all later!'

A campaign office was soon established in the church hall. Mary settled down to draw the area around the library and the Town Hall and Beth started typing up dates and times. Clo and Lizzie nailed cardboard onto wooden slats from old fruit boxes and painted them with white emulsion, courtesy of Ginny.

'Exactly which way are we marching on the day?' Mary asked, looking up from her drawing.

'Yes, we need to know as soon as possible,' said Beth, pausing in her typing.

'I'm not sure yet,' said Clo, 'we've got to get permission.'

She sploshed white paint onto another placard.

'I hope you're not getting that paint on the linoleum, girls!' Mrs Thorne hovered on the stairs, duster in hand.

'No, Mrs Thorne,' said Clo, 'we've put some newspaper down.'

'Good girl. It's a very charitable thing that you're doing,' she declared, solemnly, 'helping the afflicted what can't help themselves. The Lord will bless you for it.'

She went back upstairs polishing the banister as she went.

The girls giggled.

'You will be very blessed, my child,' pronounced Lizzie and dabbed Clo on the forehead with her paintbrush.

'Hey, watch it,' spluttered Clo, emulsion paint running down her nose.

'Leave it on, you won't need any make-up for the demo!' laughed Beth.

Howard appeared in a hurry.

'Clo, we have to go down to the police station at once,' he said. 'Good grief, child, you've gone quite white!'

'It's only paint,' said Clo.

'I was afraid it might be. Wash it off, there's a good girl—
we must go and discuss our route with the police and get their
approval.'

Clo dashed into the Ladies, stuck her head under the tap
and tried to get the paint out of her hair. She was only partly
successful.

Ten minutes later she and Howard entered Rushworth
Central Police Station. The Sergeant was expecting them and
took them through to the back.

'We're not too late to apply for a permit, are we?' Howard
asked.

Clo's heart missed a beat. What if they couldn't get
permission after all?

Sergeant Atkins unfolded a large map.

'Oh no,' he said, 'so long as we have a clear week's notice
we can cope, and there's every likelihood you'll get the go-
ahead anyway. We only refuse something that might cause a
breach of the peace. You weren't planning anything
inflammatory, were you, Miss?'

'Well I hope it will make people want to go and do
something,' Clo said.

'Like what, exactly?' The Sergeant looked stern.

'Well, make sure disabled people can get into places and
treat them like human beings...' Clo faltered.

'Nothing dangerous, like?'

'Oh no.'

Sergeant Atkins chuckled. 'That's all right then! Now, let's
decide on a route. I suggest you leave Library Square by
Market Street and proceed, in an orderly fashion, of course,
up Carter Gate...'

By the time they left the police station everything was
agreed, and Clo glowed with importance—now they were
official, it was really going to happen!

The week passed in a flurry of phone calls, posters,
placards and petitions, and suddenly it was Friday again.
There were more people at the meeting this time, including
Jenny, the Lewis girls, Mrs Avery and Mr Rashid.

'Much of the forward planning is done,' Howard told them,
'we have the blessing of the local police...' he waved a piece of
paper and everybody cheered, '... and Sergeant Atkins will
come along the night before to give us last-minute
instructions. Now we need to look at the details. How is the
banner coming along, Mrs Avery?'

'Very well, thank you. My ladies caught the vision, as you might say, and are hard at it even as we speak. We hope to provide you with something rather special.'

'Thank you for going to so much trouble.'

'Oh we're enjoying it; it's a challenge to do something different at such short notice.'

'How about the placards?'

Lizzie showed them one with 'No Laughing Matter' painted on it.

'We've done fifteen big ones like this and we'll do some more,' she said. 'The playgroups are getting the children to make theirs so there should be plenty.'

'Good thinking,' said Howard. 'Miss Redmond, how are things your end?'

'Fine. I've got three friends from Rushworth Dramatic Society and Angel from Food for Thought to do the make-up. Did you fix up St Joseph's?'

'Yes, Father Dennis was delighted to help. We can meet and change and get made-up in their hall and he said they'll even lay on refreshments.'

'I've been into school to see about the Public Address equipment,' continued Miss Redmond, 'and, fingers crossed, Mr James will come and set it up for us.'

'And I've got the band OK,' said Isaac, 'the guys can't wait! My mate Gussy plays a wicked saxophone, he'll grab people's attention.'

An elegantly-dressed black lady appeared on the stairs.

'And this here is my mum,' Isaac introduced her, 'she wants to help too.'

'Things are a bit slack at the moment,' Mrs Johnson explained, 'so if you wants any sewing doing, I'm your woman.'

Howard turned to Clo.

'If we're doing the clown thing,' she said, 'I thought we could ask everybody to wear bright or silly clothes and then get ruffs to go round their necks. Could you make some ruffs, Mrs Johnson?'

'Sure, honey, no problem, how many you want—fifty, a hundred?'

'As many as you can manage, I think,' said Miss Redmond. 'We'll have to buy some fabric.'

'There I can help you,' said Mr Rashid, 'I will supply all you need. What would you like?'

'Something really bright, please,' said Clo.

'I have a roll of particularly vivid orange at the moment,' Mr Rashid said, 'not unlike the colour of your posters! Is that the sort of thing?'

'That sounds most suitable!' laughed Ginny. 'Thank you, Mr Rashid, you've been very good and I'm determined to buy a sari from you for our house-warming—if we ever move. Shall I call round for the material tomorrow?'

'I will be delighted to see you,' said Mr Rashid with a little bow. 'I am doing all I can to advertise this campaign. I have taken the liberty of translating the information into Hindi, Gujerati and Punjabi for those who do not read very good English. My friend Mr Wing has also promised to write it in Chinese on his shop window.'

'Excellent!' said Howard, 'I'd never have thought of that.'

'Many are denied access simply because they cannot read the language,' said Mr Rashid.

'Now, the speeches,' said Howard, 'how far have we got with those?'

Clo glanced at Miss Redmond, who smiled encouragingly.

'I'm going to announce things,' she said, 'say who we are, why we're there and what we're going to do. Then I'll introduce the other speakers.'

'And they are... ?' Howard asked, pencil poised.

'Er, I'm not sure yet,' Clo confessed.

'Let's see if we can decide between us,' Howard said, 'who do you think?'

'Well, someone from Whitegates, and someone who's old, and someone with little kids, that sort of thing.'

'OK. Mrs Giddins, would you be prepared to speak?'

'Just try and stop me. What with spending cuts and so on, I'll do anything to bring our children's needs to people's notice.'

'Mrs Giddins for one,' Howard wrote down, 'and someone elderly? Mrs Appleby's not with us this evening.'

'No, they're flat-hunting again,' said Beth. 'Her old people are a bit frail for standing up and making speeches. What about your Mrs Wilkins, Clo?'

'I'll ask her,' said Clo, 'she's doing ever so well collecting names outside Savemore's.'

'Right,' said Howard, 'Mrs Wilkins is a possible. Playgroups?'

'I'll see if I can persuade Muriel Jones,' said Ginny, 'she's hoping to stand for the Council next time and as the mother of young twins she's got plenty to say on the subject! I'll give her a ring.'

'It would be good to have somebody from the Asian community—Mr Rashid?'

'I am no good at speeches,' said Mr Rashid, 'But Abdul's health visitor, Meja, might agree. She is a very articulate young woman. I will ask.'

'Is that enough?' Howard asked.

'Not quite,' said Clo. 'Somebody who's actually disabled should speak—apart from Mrs Wilkins, I mean.'

'Couldn't agree more,' said Mrs Giddins, 'we mustn't fall into the trap of speaking *for* disabled people and never letting them speak for themselves. There's been too much of that in the past.'

'Will you do it, Beth?' Clo asked.

Beth shook her head. 'I don't think it should be me. I think it ought to be someone who's quite severely disabled—like Gary.'

'I think you're right, but nobody would understand what he was saying, would they? It takes a while to get used to him,' said Clo.

'Let him have an interpreter then,' said Howard, 'if he was a foreign visitor you would, so why not let him speak for himself and get someone to translate? What do you think, Mrs Giddins?'

'I think it's the best idea so far. Our Gary is a young man with plenty to say,' said Mrs Giddins. 'He'll love it and Jane, his helper, would interpret.'

'Better tell her to leave out his jokes then!' said Clo.

'Yes I know what you mean!' laughed Mrs Giddins.

'Good.' Howard consulted his list. 'I think we've covered everything. Ginny will collect the material from Mr Rashid tomorrow and bring it to you, Mrs Johnson. Mrs Avery, thank your ladies for their hard work and say we look forward to the banner enormously. Clo's team, carry on as you have been doing and step up the petitioning. Maps and instructions must be in the post next week so make sure we've got all the addresses. Oh, and Jenny, isn't it? Sorry, I almost forgot you. Anything to report?'

'Only that I've been ringing round people to push wheelchairs on the day and so far I've got seven for definite and four more possibles,' Jenny said.

'Thank you,' Howard said, 'that will be a great help. Clo,

perhaps you'd pass that on to Mabel? Good. Want to add anything, Kim?'

'Only to keep up the momentum,' Kim said, 'it's important we don't flag now. Encourage one another.'

'Excellent advice,' said Howard, 'it might be applied to our moving plans as well. If we ever do move into the Wreck— sorry, the Manse, next door, you'll all be invited to the party.'

'If you want any help, man, just give me a call,' said Isaac.

'Me too,' said Miss Redmond, 'I'll help.'

'And me,' said Kim.

'Thanks, everybody, that's really good of you.'

'Well, we won't know what to do with ourselves when this is all over,' said Kim. 'Don't leave without a poster and some leaflets, everybody.'

Outside Miss Redmond said to Beth, 'I was in the school office yesterday and the secretary was asking whether you'll be fit to come back next term.'

'I hope so. Will they let me come in a wheelchair? I've missed nearly a whole year.'

'Yes, I'm afraid you may have to stay down a year to catch up, we'll need to discuss all that .The only alternative is home tuition which, I'm afraid, is rather inadequate. As for the wheelchair—well, access is the name of the game, isn't it?'

'Of course!'

'Tell your granny Mrs Cooper will phone her next week,' said Miss Redmond, 'we want you back as soon as possible.'

'Hear, hear!' said Jenny, catching the end of the conversation. 'Can I push you home, Beth? I need to practise before the demo, or I'll be tipping some poor old gentleman into the gutter!'

19

With only four days to go to the demonstration, everybody seemed preoccupied with something else. Clo and Lizzie hung about the pottery wondering what to do. All the posters had been stuck up, instructions sent off, and the church hall was overflowing with placards bearing slogans like, 'Rushworth Says Disabled Access NOW!' and 'Don't Leave Us Out in the Cold'. The Sunday School teachers had passed a few comments about never mind being left *out*, their classes couldn't even squeeze *in* amongst all the campaign paraphernalia.

'And it's No Laughing Matter,' said one, dryly, 'when you've got thirty children squashed into a space the size of a large loo—not in this hot weather!'

Isaac and Kim were packing the kiln for a firing before the weekend.

'Shan't have time Friday or Saturday,' said Kim, 'but we must keep production ticking over.'

Isaac groaned, 'Don't talk to me 'bout production, man, my mum can't think of nothing but them clown things. I had to go down the chippy last night. She's doing no cooking, she says, till after the demonstration.'

'You'll survive!' Kim laughed.

Lizzie ran her finger idly along the incense-stick stand and it came off furry with dust; like a lot of other routine jobs, cleaning had been neglected of late.

'It's a bit dusty in here,' she said loudly in the direction of the bead curtain.

'Then dust it, dear Lizzie, dear Lizzie, dear Lizzie!' chanted Kim over the clatter of pots.

'All right.' She got the feather duster from under the counter and flicked it idly over the window display.

'What shall we do?' she said. 'Can't go home. Mum and Dad are flying around like mad things—they *hope* we're going to move next week. Everything keeps getting packed and then unpacked when we need it again, it's awful. Come to think of it, I haven't seen Joel for a while—he's probably been packed.'

'Ha ha. It's about the same round the flat,' Clo said, picking dead flies out of the planters, 'they haven't said anything, but Eric's started collecting cardboard boxes and chucking things out. Mam went off in her best clothes this morning saying something about getting references but she wouldn't tell me what for.'

'You must be moving too.'

'We've got to be out the flat by the end of the month so I jolly well hope so; I don't know what we'll do if we don't find somewhere in time.'

'You can come and live with us, the Wreck's enormous.'

'That would be nice. Where's Mary?'

'Taken Beth to the park to practise.'

'She's determined to go back to school next term. She's going to start Year 10 again in Mary's class.'

'Doesn't she mind?'

'No, she says she wouldn't mind going back in Year 7 with the babies, so long as she goes back.'

'It's amazing how much she's changed,' said Lizzie. 'You too, you sounded pretty desperate when you wrote to me in Brinkley.'

'I was,' said Clo, 'it was just awful. Everything seemed to be against us and it felt like I had to bear it all on my own.'

'What happened?'

'Lots of things; finding out there are people who understand, like your mum and dad; and that even if there's no one else around you can always talk to... God about it. Doing something positive, this campaign, that's helped. Do you know, me and Beth weren't even speaking to each other a couple of weeks ago? We were both so angry and unhappy. Things are much better now.'

'That's great. Mum says Beth's swimming's improving too.'

'Yes it is, she's talking about getting involved in sports for the disabled—did you know there's even a disabled Olympics?'

The shop bell jingled.

'Parcel for Miss C. Olerenshaw,' said the delivery man.

'Oh. That's me,' said Clo.

'Sign here then.'

She turned the box over, excitedly. 'It's from Acme Advertising—500 balloons, it says. Hey, we've got balloons!'

'And every one printed with Open Up Rushworth! in glorious Technicolor,' Kim said, coming through. 'Yes, I ordered them.'

'Did they cost a lot of money?' Clo asked anxiously.

'Don't worry. Anonymous donor.'

'Great,' said Lizzie, 'I love balloons, let's have a go.'

She blew hard into a pink one which inflated to the size of a tennis ball.

'Phew, I haven't got enough puff!'

'Don't worry,' said Kim. 'St Joseph's have still got the helium cylinder they had for their fête last week, so if you'd like to pop them over to Sister Maureen at their office, she's promised to have them all inflated and waiting for us on Saturday morning.'

They found St Joseph's office behind the church and rang the bell. A young nun with a broad grin opened the door.

'Ah, you've brought the balloons for Saturday, smashing, we'll see to them for you. Which one of you is Chloe then?'

'That's me and this is Lizzie Lewis,' Clo said.

'Well,' said Sister Maureen. 'you're both doing a fine job and we'll be marching with you on Saturday.'

'*Really?*'

'Oh yes, nuns aren't a lot of old holy relics shut away from the real world, not our lot anyway. See you Saturday!'

'Gosh, nuns as well,' said Lizzie as they went down the steps, 'there'll be a fair old mixture and no mistake.'

'What now?' said Clo. 'Fancy spying out the land for Saturday?'

'What, the library, you mean?'

'Yes, shall we?'

'OK. Watch out for dragons though!'

They crept round the side of the building. The fire door was open for ventilation but there was a piece of string across, with a hand-written notice hanging from it which said, No Public Admittance.

'Tee hee, that won't be there much longer,' sniggered Lizzie, 'shall we pinch it now?'

'Lizzie Lewis!' giggled Clo, 'I'm shocked to hear you suggest such a thing, and you a minister's daughter! It's tempting though.'

They slipped past and climbed the steps.

'One, two, three...' Clo counted, 'there's fifteen steps up—absolutely useless! Thing is, I'm not sure how they could alter them, are you?'

'How about a ski-lift?' suggested Lizzie. 'There must be a way. Where are you doing the speeches from?'

'Down the bottom. That's a public right of way. If we stand on the steps the Dragon might have us arrested for obstruction.'

'You need a soap box, that's what they use. Dad took us to hear an old fellow at Hyde Park in London once. His name was Lord Soaper so I expect he started it.'

'I don't think soap comes in those sort of boxes any more.'

'Phew, it's hot. Shall we go for a milk shake? I've got some money.'

'Good idea.'

As they made their way to Gino's a familiar figure with pink hair was wheeled into view—Mrs Wilkins, clutching a pile of papers and looking extremely cross, pushed briskly along by her daughter Iris.

'Chloe Olerenshaw!' Mrs Wilkins cried as they drew level, 'I'm being kidnapped! Tell this stupid girl I've got a job of work to do, I've got names to collect, it's important!'

It took Clo a moment to realize that the stupid girl was Iris who was almost as old as Mam.

'I know it's important, Mother,' Iris said, 'but you've been sat outside Savemore's for over a week, you need a rest. Anyway the customers are getting fed up of you grabbing them to sign up for the fourth or fifth time.'

'I can't help that, I can't see as well as I used to,' grumbled Mrs Wilkins, 'but you've no right to remove me like that, just because I'm a helpless old woman in a wheelchair. You wait my girl, things are about to change!'

Iris pinched her lips together and said nothing.

'I'm glad I've seen you, Mrs Wilkins,' Clo said, 'because I wanted to ask you if you'll say something at the demonstration. You will be there, won't you?'

'Just try and stop me,' giggled the old lady, 'what do you want me to say?'

'Only a few words, about how difficult it is getting into places...'

'When you're an old crock like me. I know,' said Mrs Wilkins, cheerfully. 'I'll be there, duckie, no fear. I've told all me pals at the Over Sixties Club as well.'

'Thanks, that's brilliant. Are those petitions you've got there?'

'Yes, you'd better have them. I reckon there's nigh on three hundred names here—there might be a few on twice but don't tell anybody. There'd be a whole lot more if I hadn't been hijacked!'

She screwed her head round to scowl at Iris who made a face at Clo and Lizzie before wheeling her mother rapidly away.

Later Clo presented herself at Miss Redmond's flat.

'Come in, Chloe, make yourself at home,' said Miss Redmond, 'cup of tea?'

'Yes, please.'

While she waited Clo admired the things in Miss Redmond's front room. A bronze bust of Shakespeare sported a beaded hat and sat on a piece of oriental embroidery; the remains of a joss stick crumbled soft grey ash into a brass holder; and there were a number of pots that looked like Kim's handiwork about the place. Clo recognized the special turquoise-blue raku pot she had so admired the first time they went to the pottery.

'I'm glad she's got it, anyway,' she thought, 'she'll take care of it.'

'Recognize the pottery?' Miss Redmond said, coming into the room with the tea.

Jasmine tea, Clo noticed, an Aquarius Pots speciality.

'Can't think how I never discovered it before, it has a quality all of its own. Kim Bell is a very talented potter.' She blushed slightly.

'Now, to business. Stand at the other end of the room, Chloe, and breathe from your diaphragm, as I taught you for the play.'

She handed Clo an artificial chrysanthemum to use as a microphone.

'Loud and clear. Don't hold the mike directly in front of your mouth and don't wave it about. Read ahead, and look up as much as you possibly can, people hear you better if they can see your face, especially at a distance.'

It was just like being back at school!

Self-consciously Clo began, chrysanthemum in one hand, notes in the other.

'No, no, no!' Miss Redmond interrupted, 'You mustn't apologize! You've got every right to be there, remember.'

Clo tried again, managing this time to sound like Mrs Cooper doing the announcements in Assembly.

'Stop! You're not doing "Friends, Romans, countrymen"! This isn't the same as acting, Chloe, you can't hide behind a character. You must project *yourself*, that's who we want to hear. Try it again—as Chloe Olerenshaw this time.'

She made Clo do it over and over again until she was satisfied.

At last she smiled. 'Good, I think that will do. Are you nervous?'

'Yes.'

'That's no bad thing. A few nerves get the adrenaline flowing and give energy to your performance, remember the play?'

'Yes, Miss, that was great! Oh—Miss?'

'Yes?'

'Won't I need something to stand on? Lizzie says I need a soap box.'

'I'd already thought of that. Mr James is bringing a small rostrum from school. He can pack it straight back into his car with the PA equipment when you start marching so it shouldn't get in anybody's way.'

'Thanks, Miss, that's everything then.'

Miss Redmond saw Clo to the door.

'I'm going to the theatrical shop with Angel tomorrow to buy greasepaint for the clowns. Apparently face-painting, as they call it, is very popular at the music festivals she goes to, she's quite an old hand at it.'

'Isn't greasepaint expensive?'

'Yes, but it goes a long way. Let's just say that it's my contribution. See you at the meeting on Friday night. After that it will be all systems go! Bye!'

20

Clo was awake with the birds. Saturday at last!

She reached under her pillow for her notes and went over her speech again and again until the alarm went off.

'Wassa time?' mumbled Beth from underneath the bedclothes.

'Seven.'

'What's it like out?'

Clo padded over to the window and pulled back the curtains. A thin white mist hovered over Raglan Street.

'Dry, and sort of shimmery, it'll probably be hot.'

'Eric said there were thunderstorms forecast,' Beth said, poking her head out.

'Please God,' Clo prayed silently, 'I don't know if you're there, but today is really important. Please, *please* don't let it rain till the march is over, about 12.30 should be fine. Thanks. Oh, and please let me get this speech right! Amen.'

Mam came in with a tray of tea. 'Here you are, little treat, though why you need to go so early I don't know.'

'Loads to do, Mam,' said Clo blowing on the hot tea, 'we've got to get all the placards and stuff to St Joseph's by nine, then there's the clown things to collect from Mrs Johnson's— she's made some hats as well, with pom-poms on them—then I've got to see Mr James to find out how the microphones work—oh, lots of things.'

Mam was convinced. 'Alright then, breakfast in half an hour—a proper cooked one because you might not get any lunch. Eric'll drive you over in good time.'

Clo jumped out of bed and dressed. First, a yellow T-shirt with letters stuck on the back saying Open Up NOW! and a huge sunflower on the front, then the red leggings with black stars, her old trainers with the toes cut out and her Rasta hat with plaits made of orange knitting wool sewn on.

'Go away, you look like Blackpool Illuminations!' Beth groaned.

She put on her pink dress, shiny blue dance tights and a battered top hat from Clo's hoard with a plastic daffodil stuck in the brim.

'You do look a pair,' exclaimed Mam, as she kissed them good-bye, 'like something out of the circus! Now we may not see you again till the end so God bless. We'll meet you at St Joseph's after. We've got something to show you.'

'What, Mam?' asked Clo.

'Never you mind, it'll keep. Take care now.'

Eric dropped Clo off at the church hall where Howard and Isaac were already loading up.

'I found some streamers and things left over from Christmas,' Howard said, adding a box to the van, 'might as well use them. Right-oh Isaac, you take this lot to St Joseph's. Clo, come with me, we have to find a hardware shop.'

Thompson's Hardware was in Brickfields, a few doors from Mr Eccles'. Howard leapt out and returned a few minutes later with two wooden broom handles.

'What are they for?' Clo asked.

'Wait and see,' he said, 'all will be revealed ere long.'

Mr Eccles was arranging newspapers in the rack outside his door.

'All the best to you this morning,' he said, 'I shall see you t'other end. I'm closing early on purpose.'

A notice on the door said 'Owing to urgent Council business this shop will be closed between 10.45 a.m. and 12.30 p.m. today. We apologize for any inconvenience caused.'

'Oh, and wait a minute.'

He disappeared inside and came back with some copies of the petition.

'You'll want these. Any idea how many names you've got so far?'

'Well,' said Clo, 'you get thirty to a sheet and we've collected eighty sheets up to now.'

'There's another six there, so I reckon that's in the region of two and a half thousand, and you'll get more this morning. A very respectable amount, that.'

'Thanks,' said Clo, 'see you later.'

'You certainly will!' He slapped the top of the car and waved them off.

'He'll be at the Town Hall when we arrive,' Clo said, 'that'll be nice, won't it?'

'Yes, grand,' said Howard. 'Ginny rang the TV studios. Don't know if they'll come but you never know.'

Clo shivered with excitement.

As they drew up outside St Joseph's people were already

arriving. Mums and dads with babies in pushchairs and slings were chatting together. Most of the children had their faces painted like animals with whiskers.

'We did that ourselves,' said one of the women, proudly, 'and these, look.'

They showed Clo a pile of colourful placards obviously drawn by children.

Inside the hall there were wheelchairs everywhere. Miss Redmond and her team were going round applying big red grins and funny eyebrows. Mrs Johnson, her mouth full of pins, was attaching frilly orange ruffs to all and sundry and Sister Maureen's team were dispensing cups of tea and balloons, whichever seemed most appropriate. Kim was threading streamers through the spokes of someone's wheels.

'Hi, Clo!' he called. 'Everything's under control, sixty minutes to go and counting!'

Mr James came across, screwdriver in one hand, microphone in the other and a cup of tea balanced between the two.

'Good morning, Chloe, I believe you are responsible for this production? Ten sharp outside the library to test the sound, all right?'

'But first of all, you gotta be painted like everyone else!' Angel, resplendent in multi-coloured rags and tinsel in her hair seized Clo.

'Sit down,' she ordered, 'and don't fidget.'

Clo sat.

Ginny drifted by in a mauve sari with Joel on her hip clutching a bunch of balloons.

Jane pushed Gary over to say that he could only think of half an hour's worth of speech, was that enough?

'He's joking—I hope!' she said and wheeled him away to be made up.

'OK, you can look now.' Angel produced a hand mirror. 'It's a traditional White Face clown make-up,' she told Clo, 'he's the serious one in the sequins who's in charge. But I've given you a special star as well.'

A silver star shone on Clo's right cheek.

'And that's because you are one—you're a real star, kid. My mum had a horrible accident and got paralyzed and it was really hard for her never to be able to go to the pictures or concerts again. She'd have been really pleased somebody was doing something about it.'

'Is she... ?'

'Yeah, she died two years ago. Too late for Mum but not too late for all these. See you later.'

She bounded off to help Isaac who had Howard pinned laughing to the wall.

'Even vicars have to be made up!' she yelled, 'hold him down, man!'

At ten o'clock Clo went round to Library Square with Kim. He wore enormous trousers suspended from rainbow braces, threaded with a wire hoop so that they billowed around him like a ship in full sail. People were beginning to gather and there were whistles and cheers when they appeared. At their heels pranced Daffy, sporting an orange ruff with sequins on it.

'Stand up there,' said Mr James pointing Clo to a small platform.

He retreated to a spot about twenty yards away.

'Now try speaking into the mike,' he called.

'What shall I say?' she asked.

Her voice echoed back to her across the Square and the spectators laughed.

'That's fine!' shouted Mr James, running back. 'Just remember—"no half measures", eh?'

Isaac's friend Gussy arrived, and soon the sound of a soulful saxophone filled the Square as more and more people gathered. A young woman with long black hair, wearing a pink jogging suit, introduced herself as Meja and took her place beside the platform. Mary wheeled Beth over.

'Good luck, Clo,' Beth said. 'Is everybody here?'

Clo consulted her list: 'Meja; yes. Gary; yes. Mrs Giddins; yes, I've seen her.'

A woman with a double buggy containing twins, their faces painted like a pair of small tigers, arrived.

'Hello, I'm Muriel Jones,' she said.

Clo ticked her off on the list.

Howard appeared, duly painted, his dog collar looking rather peculiar worn with floral dungarees and a ginger wig.

'Who's missing?' he asked.

'No Mrs Wilkins yet. She said she'd be here. Oh dear, I hope Iris isn't holding her prisoner!'

Even as she spoke, they heard an urgent hooting and, 'Let me through, I'm a speaker!'

The crowd parted and Mrs Wilkins, perched on a sort of three-wheeled motor scooter, drove erratically to the front.

'Here we are, my duckie! Isn't this grand? I'm glad I got it in time.'

'It's wonderful, Mrs Wilkins,' Clo said, stepping out of the way, 'you can lead the pensioners in the march.'

'They won't be able to keep up with me!' cackled Mrs Wilkins. 'Oh, thanks dearie,' as Lizzie tied a couple of balloons to her handlebars.

'Right,' said Howard by Clo's side, 'that's everybody. Heavenly Father, we pray that you will be marching with us this morning and that justice may be done. OK, let's get this show on the road!'

Gussy rounded off his performance with some extravagant trills and stepped down, smiling broadly, to applause.

'Your turn, sister,' he said to Clo, 'I warmed 'em up for you!'

Clutching her precious notes Clo mounted the platform. She gazed across the Square: there were people as far as she could see, many in costume, a lot of them in wheelchairs. She saw Mr and Mrs Rashid and their friends, and the children from Whitegates having the time of their lives with party poppers and blowers. She turned her head and looked up the library steps; there were faces at all the windows and she could have sworn she saw the Dragon glaring down at her. So many people, all waiting for her to speak. She felt giddy.

'Help!' she prayed.

Clutching the microphone for support, she cleared her throat.

'People of Rushworth,' she began, 'we are the Open Up Campaign and we are here to draw your attention to the problems faced every day by people in wheelchairs, people with pushchairs and people who just can't get around so well. Behind me you can see our public library; it is a very good library but you have to climb fifteen steps to get into it. That's fine if you are strong and healthy but no good if you're not. Look around you. Many people amongst us today have no hope at all of ever using this library... '

There were cries of 'Hear, hear', 'She's right, you know!' and 'Time summat was done!'

Clo became aware that some of these cries were coming from behind her. She looked round; a figure was hobbling down the steps waving a walking stick.

'She's right, she's right, you listen to her!' cried Ernie Earnshaw.

Quite undeterred by the size of his audience he stood and shouted, 'And what's more, there's a side entrance what you're not allowed to use neither, it's a crime and a shame!' before hobbling down the rest of the steps into the crowd.

Clo was completely thrown for a moment.

'Er, thank you,' she said. 'It was Mr Earnshaw who first pointed out to me that there is a door at ground level but it can't be used because of the rules—we need new rules, to let people in, not keep them out!'

The crowd cheered.

'And now...'

She had lost her place; her mouth went dry and she felt panic rising. Then someone was at her elbow: it was Howard and she was on course again.

'... the Reverend Howard Lewis of Rushworth Methodist Church will say a few words.'

Trembling, she handed the microphone to Howard who put his hand over it and whispered, 'Great stuff, Clo, you didn't say you'd set up that old boy to put in his two penn'orth.'

'I didn't...' she said, but Howard was already addressing the crowd.

This gave her a chance to sort out her notes and when Howard had finished she gave out the information she had been about to impart when Ernie made his surprise appearance.

'We shall be marching to the Town Hall via Market Street and Carter Gate in about twenty minutes, and in the meantime people will be coming round with our petition. Please sign it now if you haven't already.'

She introduced Mrs Giddins and sat down on the steps. Daffy squirmed through the sea of legs and stationed himself beside her. Clo hugged him.

Meja spoke next with great clarity, saying how problems of access affected all races and classes and ages, and that the different communities must all work together to remedy it. Her appeal was warmly received.

Muriel Jones made a great pantomime of demonstrating how to get a twin buggy up the steps with the twins giggling and shouting as they were bumped up and down and everyone laughed.

Then she took the platform and said, 'But seriously ladies and gentlemen, any woman with small children here will tell

149

you how difficult it is trying to shop or do anything with a buggy or a pram.'

The playgroup contingent yelled agreement.

'Granted,' said Muriel, 'a few dads here do experience the same problems but it's my opinion that these conditions continue to exist because most town planners and architects are *men* and it's not usually them who have to cope with the result. Councillors and planners *must* consult the people who mainly use these facilities—women, old people and children!'

More cheering and a few cat calls.

Clo noticed a flash gun go off and saw somebody near the front with a tape recorder. Howard nudged her. 'The Press are here.'

Gary was the real star of the show. He was hoisted up onto the platform and his chair held steady by several strong men. Mr James produced a second microphone for Jane who perched beside him.

'This is Gary Smith, ladies and gentlemen,' she said, 'a skilled computer operator, writer, composer and something of a comedian. He has plenty to say for himself and if you were to spend time with him you would soon be able to understand him but, for today, I will be Gary's interpreter. Over to you, Gary.'

Gary waved to the crowd, took the microphone and, with a supreme effort of concentration, managed to hold it still enough to speak into.

'Hello, I'm Gary,' Jane interpreted, 'I've got cerebral palsy: don't worry, it isn't catching. Did you hear about the disabled man who couldn't go dancing? He had a flat tyre!'

There was a sprinkling of nervous laughter.

'It's all right, you can laugh,' said Gary, 'you have to laugh or you'd chuck yourself in the canal—only in my case I'd have to ring up and make an appointment three weeks in advance! Daft, isn't it? But there's hundreds of people like me in Rushworth who can't use the basic amenities able-bodied people take for granted. It's not on! It's indefensible! These town planners don't have a leg to stand on—like me really!'

He went on in this vein, cracking jokes to make his point all the more forcibly. As he was lifted down the crowd roared support and several wiped away a tear.

Mrs Wilkins spoke last and told them how wonderful it was for her to have her new scooter, because it gave her a choice about where she went instead of being literally pushed around by other people.

Clo took the stage for the last time.

'Now we are going to march to the Town Hall to deliver our petition for disabled access in Rushworth. Please follow the Open Up banner...'

She looked round for it.

On the steps behind her Howard and Kim unfurled a piece of blue material about eight feet long and three feet wide fastened at either end to a broom handle. The words, OPEN UP RUSHWORTH shone in gold edged with scarlet. They were superimposed over black bars through which many hands stretched; one hand held a crutch, another a rattle, black hands, brown hands, white hands, old hands, babies' hands, all pleading to be let in. A gasp of admiration went up and cameras flashed.

Clo forgot she still held the microphone and exclaimed, 'Oh! That's brilliant, Mrs Avery!'

Kim and Howard led the way to the far end of the Square where the steel band waited. People organized themselves behind and Sergeant Atkins himself stopped the traffic to let them out into Market Street. The procession moved slowly but exuberantly; people came out of the shops and waved from upstairs windows and motorists hooted in solidarity.

First came the wonderful banner flashing in the sunshine, then the band in carnival costume, dancing and carrying their drums like upturned dustbin lids before them, and Gussy, blowing his saxophone for all he was worth. Next came the Whitegates youngsters led by Gary, and Mrs Giddins with a megaphone, leading a chant of, 'Let us in, in-in-in!' Behind them came Mrs Wilkins, tooting her horn, the residents of the Homestead and many more elderly people; Clo saw Mrs Thorne pushing a lady in a hat that looked like a whole flower stall. Mr Rashid and his friends came next, dignified and brightly dressed with Abdul and several other children and old people in chairs. Some nuns followed, wimples flying, arm in arm with Angel and a group of punks sporting crests of green and red hair and gleaming studded jackets. Bringing up the rear were the playgroup people with toddlers and babies stretching back as far as the eye could see.

Lizzie grabbed Clo. 'There's a film crew over the other side, come and see!'

They wove and ducked through the procession.

'It's Mum's friend Alan—hi, Al!'

The cameraman turned round. 'Hi there, sweetheart! You see we came, your mama threatened me with sudden death if we didn't!'

'This is my friend Clo, who invented it all,' said Lizzie.

'Really? Pleased to meet you, Clo, smile please.' Alan turned the camera on her. 'Watch the news tonight, girls, we'll try and get you on.'

'Gosh, us on the telly,' said Clo, 'I can't believe it!'

The front of the march was approaching the Town Hall.

'Get the petition together,' Kim said, 'we're nearly there. Ginny's got the rest of it.'

They located Ginny by her glittering sari, among the playgroupers.

'Where is it, Mum?' Lizzie demanded: Ginny's hands were empty.

'You haven't forgotten it, have you?' Clo asked anxiously.

'Trust me!' said Ginny. 'Joel's got it.'

'Wha-at?'

'He's sitting on it,' she said, unstrapping the baby who was beginning to grizzle and tug at his orange ruff. 'Just hope he hasn't done anything unfortunate on it.'

She lifted him out to reveal the petition stacked neatly under the seat of his pushchair.

'No, you're in luck, it's quite dry!'

Clo and Lizzie seized the pile of paper and carried it to the front, collecting more sheets on the way.

'Quick, count the extras,' Kim said.

'Eighteen,' said Lizzie.

'Right. Eighteen times thirty equals five hundred and forty, plus the two and a half thousand we've got already—I reckon we've topped three thousand signatures.'

The procession had come to a standstill in front of an imposing building with huge oak doors studded with brass. The crowd went quiet, waiting for something to happen.

'Come on,' said Howard, propelling Clo and Lizzie up the steps.

He rang a bell and a man in uniform poked his head through a little hatch in the door. They stood back to wait for Mr Eccles. Then, to their surprise, the oak doors were thrown open and no less a person than the Lord Mayor of Rushworth, in full regalia and gold chain of office, stepped forward.

The Mayor said in a loud voice, 'And what can I do for you?'

Clo thought, 'He must know why we're here.'

But when Mr James darted in front of them with the microphone, she realized that they were expected to put on some kind of show for the spectators.

Clo rose to the occasion. 'I come on behalf of the people of Rushworth,' she said clearly, 'disabled people, old people, children, to appeal to you to make improved access to all public buildings a priority. This petition contains over three thousand names to support it.'

Gravely the Mayor took the pile from Clo and handed it to Mr Eccles, who winked at her. 'On behalf of Rushworth Town Council,' he said, 'I accept this petition, and promise that it will be given every attention in the near future.'

He shook Clo's hand, posed for the cameras, then turned and went back inside. The oak doors swung silently to behind him. People began to drift away.

'Is that it then?' Clo asked Kim.

'Yes, that's it, you've done it. It remains to be seen what *they* do about it but somehow I don't think they'll be able to ignore it.'

Clo sat down on the steps. All she could say was, 'Oh.'

Daffy jumped up and planted an encouraging lick on her nose.

Miss Redmond joined them. 'Have you seen Beth?' she asked excitedly.

Clo tried to locate her sister in the dispersing crowd. 'No, why?'

'Over there by the flower tubs,' Miss Redmond pointed.

'Oh. Yes!'

Beth stood talking to Jenny and Mary and Derek Gibson. She had one hand on the back of her wheelchair, but you would never have known there was anything the matter with her.

'She walked most of the way,' said Kim, 'Mary told me. She's been practising. That girl's well on the way to recovery. She won't need that chair much longer.'

'That's brilliant!' said Clo.

'Isn't it!' agreed Kim.

'You know, I used to think of her as an albatross—like the one in the 'Ancient Mariner'—a great weight round my neck.'

'Not now?'

'Oh no. The albatross was dead. Beth's alive.'

'And flying,' Kim said. 'Come on, let's get back to St Joseph's, Sister Maureen's got the kettle on.'

21

Mam and Eric were waiting for them back at St Joseph's.
Mam pushed her way through the throng and scooped Clo
and Beth into her arms. She was so overcome she could
hardly speak. She held onto them both as if she would never
let them go.

'Oh my little girls,' she managed to get out, 'my own little
girls, putting all this on by yourselves, it was marvellous.'

'There were a few others, Mam,' Clo said, embarrassed.

But her grandmother took no notice. 'Oh Clo, when you
made those speeches—like you did it every day of the week!
And up at the Town Hall when you spoke to the Lord Mayor,
oh I thought I should burst!'

Clo wriggled out of Mam's embrace so that she could
breathe.

'Where were you standing? I didn't see you.'

'We saw you, though,' Eric said. 'By heck you put on a good
show, there must have been thousands of folks there. Just let
the Council try and get out of doing summat now.'

'And Beth, did you see Beth?' Clo asked.

At this Mam dissolved completely.

'Our Beth!' she wept, 'walking down Market Street good as
new... I thought I was seeing things. Praise the Lord, it's a
miracle, nothing less, that's what it is!'

Even Eric got out his handkerchief and blew his nose.

Kim edged his way through with a tray of tea and Mam
could hardly restrain herself from hugging him as well.

'Oh Mr Bell,' she said, 'I don't know how to thank you. I
confess I was over-quick to judge you and your friends at first,
but we ought never to go on appearances. What you've done
for Beth is nothing short of miraculous. Can you ever forgive
me?'

Clo squirmed but Kim handed her the tray and took Mam's
hands.

'The world is full of funny-looking people, Mrs Appleby,'
he said, 'but most of us are pretty normal underneath! I
didn't do much, I just try to return a bit of what I've received;
if a rather dotty old teacher hadn't taken me on, I'd still be in

a wheelchair today. It's been a lot of fun and I assure you there's absolutely nothing to forgive.'

He kissed Mam on both cheeks and she blushed and beamed.

'The campaign was your idea, Kim,' said Clo.

'I think you'd already begun it when we met. I was only the enabler, as it were.'

'You will let us keep coming to the pottery, won't you?' said Beth, 'I want to carry on potting.'

'Of course you can. Which reminds me, we unpacked the kiln yesterday—wait there.'

Ginny appeared looking a little dishevelled.

'You're losing your sari,' Clo said.

'Shush, Chloe!' said Mam.

'She's right!' said Ginny, 'I haven't quite got the hang of it yet. Good news, folks, we're *definitely* moving, next Wednesday!'

'At last. I am glad,' said Mam.

'Yes, at last. Invitations to the house-warming to follow shortly. We're having a curry party, Mr Rashid's cousin runs the Star of India Take-Away. Oh, hi, Kim, what have you got there?'

Kim placed a small round parcel in Beth's hands.

'Your masterpiece, Ms Olerenshaw,' he said. 'I was on tenterhooks in case it exploded or something during firing but it's fine.'

'My pot, how exciting!' Beth hugged the parcel.

'Let's see then, lovey,' Mam said.

'Yes, go on,' said Clo.

'Oh, all right.'

Beth carefully unwrapped her pot and held it up. It was unglazed earthenware with a black band round the neck, engraved with a pattern of birds; primitive, wild, swirling birds.

'It's called graffiti, this kind of decoration,' she told them.

'Sgraffito,' laughed Kim.

'Yes, er, very nice,' said Mam.

'It's beautiful,' Clo said warmly, 'you are clever.'

Beth stroked the smooth surface. 'It's my first,' she said, 'and I'll always keep it to remind me of how I started to get better.'

'Come over any time,' said Kim, 'must dash, Diana's waiting for me.'

They watched him limp swiftly to the door where Miss Redmond stood holding Daffy.

Beth looked at Clo. 'They're not...? Miss Redmond and Kim... are they?'

Clo nodded. 'I think so. I saw Kim's precious blue pot at her house—the one that he said was priceless. He must have given it to her. Funny, isn't it? They're not a bit like each other.'

'Life is full of surprises!' said Ginny.

Eric was jingling the car keys. 'Are you ready, you two? I don't want to drag you away only we need to be somewhere by half-past twelve and if we don't go now we shall be into the football traffic. I'm parked round the back.'

Clo was reluctant to leave all her friends laughing and discussing the march, but she was intrigued to know what Mam and Eric's mystery was. She gathered up her things and followed the others out to the car park. Isaac and members of the band were sitting on the wall outside, still making music for an admiring group of children.

Clo took off her hat and yanked the woollen pigtails from it.

'Here,' she said, handing it to Isaac, 'it's yours!'

'He-ey, thanks, Clo,' Isaac said, perching it on top of his sausagey hair, 'I'll keep it as a souvenir of today. Keep cool, babe!'

Eric drove out of the town centre, through Brickfields, to Moss Farm where they turned into an impressive driveway.

'Oh,' said Clo, recognizing it, 'this is The Homestead. Why have we come here, Mam, are you working today?'

'No, not today,' smiled Mam, 'wait a minute.'

Outside the main building a minibus was unloading some of the residents who had taken part in the march. Mrs Thorne saw them. She ran over and knocked on the car window and Clo wound it down.

'Very well done, girls,' she said, 'Auntie Annie did enjoy it— says she wants one of those motor scooter things now, like Mrs Wilkins! I didn't know she had it in her, ta-ta!'

Mam chuckled. 'We'll have to watch it, they'll all want one and then where shall we be?'

'Well why not?' said Clo, 'you could set up a fund.'

'I shall have to think about that.'

They drove round the corner and Eric parked outside a modern house with a neat little garden in front.

'Here we are then,' he said, getting the wheelchair out of the boot.

Mystified, Clo helped Beth out of the car.

'What do you think then?' Mam asked.

'Think?' said Clo, 'I don't know...'

Mam opened the gate and they walked up the path to a bright green front door with a shiny brass letter box and handle. A neat brass plate by the door was engraved with one word, 'Matron'.

'Come round the back a minute,' said Eric.

The Homestead had been built on the site of a big Victorian house and the garden at the back was long, merging into spacious grounds full of big old trees and rhododendron bushes. There were fruit trees and a tiny pond with water-lilies on it, and here and there a weathered stone urn or statue left over from the garden's heyday.

'Lovely,' thought Clo, 'like a tidier version of the Wreck, old and friendly.'

Mam beckoned them round to the front again and rang the bell.

'Well,' she said, 'do you think you'll like living here?'

'What?' Clo couldn't take this in.

'Mam, you don't mean it?' said Beth, 'it's lovely!'

Clo danced up and down, a bizarre sight in her streaky make-up and clown costume.

'Oh I can't believe it,' she squealed, 'a real house with an upstairs and downstairs and a proper garden! But... how did you get it?'

Mam smiled. 'You remember I told you Matron was leaving to go to Scotland? Well, I applied for the job and I got it. I only heard for sure this morning. You are looking at the new Matron of The Homestead Residential Home for the Elderly and Infirm.'

And quite uncharacteristically she did a little dance step there on the path.

'Oh Mam, that's brilliant,' said Beth, hugging her, 'but doesn't it mean a lot more work?'

'Yes, but I'll be on the spot, see? The accommodation goes with the job and that clinched it. Ah, here's Miss Evans, we can have a look inside now.'

A grey-haired lady in uniform opened the door.

'Please excuse the state of them, Matron,' Mam said, 'they've been involved in this Open Up Campaign.'

'So I hear,' said Miss Evans, 'the residents are full of it! Excuse the boxes, I've started packing.'

Later Clo and Beth sat in the back garden while Mam and Eric measured things up. They were tired and dusty, their make-up smudged and their costumes much the worse for wear. Clo stretched out on the grass beneath a tree heavy with ripe apples. Sunlight glinted and flashed through the branches.

She sighed contentedly. 'This has been the best day of my life.'

'Mine too,' said Beth.

'What, better than when you won the County Cup for gymnastics last year?'

'Much better. Walking down Market Street today felt like the greatest achievement in the world. You know, cups and medals are all very well, but they're only lumps of metal.'

'You *will* do all those things again though. Kim says you will.'

'But I'll never take them for granted, that's for sure, and when I leave school I'd like to do what he does and help kids like the ones at Whitegates.'

Clo said, 'Yes. You know how Mam says there's always somebody worse off than yourself? I thought that was just Mam being Mam. But it's true, isn't it? Today it felt like we were doing something about it. Not to get a reward, or people like Mrs Thorne to say how blessed we'll be, but just because it wants doing. Do you know what I mean?'

'Yes. Even if nothing comes of it you still have to do it. It's like running in a race really, you might not win but you have to run as if you're going to. I think that's in the Bible.'

'With all your might and no half measures. That's in the Bible too,' said Clo. 'Well, whatever comes of the Open Up Campaign, it's made people *feel* better, hasn't it, so it was worth it?'

'It has me,' Beth said, 'I don't know what I would have done otherwise.'

'You'd have got better in the end.'

'I suppose so, but it would have taken me a long time. You see, I didn't think there was anything worth living for if I couldn't run and swim and all those things. Now they don't seem quite so important after all.'

'Kim says it's who you are inside that matters, not what you can do.'

'He's right.'

Clo chewed a piece of grass. 'And there's this thing about burdens as well. Mrs Thorne makes it sound like they're something you just have to put up with, but I think they're meant to be a sort of challenge, to make you try harder.'

'Like weight-training,' said Beth. 'It makes you stronger.'

The sun disappeared behind a large cloud. Clo sat up and shivered.

'Back to school on Monday, haven't the holidays gone fast? Oh-oh, I think I felt a drop of rain.'

There was one ominous peal of thunder and the rain came down as though somebody had turned on a tap, soaking the dry grass and leaves immediately. Clo grabbed Beth's chair and they raced up the garden. They reached the porch laughing, with great spots of rain all over their clothes.

'What's the time?' Clo spluttered.

'12.45,' gasped Beth, 'why?'

Clo took off her glasses and wiped the greasy, wet hair from her face. 'Oh nothing, just wondered!'

'You *do* listen, God,' she thought, 'I know you do. Even when I was worried about the speech, the march, the weather, you had it all under control. You *do* care, about me, our family, about Rushworth and everybody in it. Thank you.' And in her heart she sang,

> Now thank we all our God
> With hearts and hands and voices,
> Who wondrous things hath done...

All Lion paperbacks are available from your local bookshop, or can be ordered direct from Lion Publishing. For a free catalogue, showing the complete list of titles available, please contact:

Customer Services Department
Lion Publishing plc
Peter's Way
Sandy Lane West
Oxford OX4 5HG

Tel: (01865) 747550
Fax: (01865) 715152